If You Play, You Must Pay

A Novel By
Luther C. Grayer

Grayer Publishing

Grayer Publishing
PO Box 788
Flossmoor, IL 60422
www.GrayerPublishing.com

Copyright © 2008 Luther C. Grayer

All rights reserved.

Without limiting the copyright reserved above, no part of this publication may be reproduced, stored in or introduced into a retrieval system, or transmitted, in any form, or by any means (electronic, mechanical, photocopying, recording, or otherwise), without prior written permission of both copyright owner and the above publisher of this book.

PUBLISHER'S NOTE
This is a work of fiction. Names, characters, places, and incidents either are the product of the author's imagination or are used fictitiously, and any resemblance to actual persons, living or dead, events, or locales is entirely coincidental.

Cover and Interior Design by
The Writer's Assistant.com

ISBN-10: 0-9785536-3-2
ISBN-13: 978-0-9785536-3-0

Visit Luther Grayer online at www.LutherGrayer.com.

Acknowledgements

Thanks to the people who bought my first novel, *The Family Grant*. I know that most of you did so as a personal favor. My wife, who was my biggest pusher, leaned on all her friends and so did I. Well, we're back again. This time with my second novel. I hope that my first one causes you to want this one, but if you didn't get around to reading the first one yet or even buying it, don't fret. Words don't spoil. You can now be on your way to becoming a collector of my works.

I am a much better salesman now than I was when my first novel was released, so I am thanking in advance those who will buy my book or books for the first time. I hope that I'm a better writer now too. Since improvement is always my goal, know that I will continue to use your comments in an attempt to get better.

Just as an added note, a story takes on significance if the storyteller has credibility. Readers want to know that what they're reading happened the way it's reported. I assure you that I was in position at all times to report accurately what occurred. I've known Andrew and other family members for their entire existence, so rest assured that I have the credentials to tell their story.

Thank you all for your support; I look forward to hearing from you. Visit www.luthergrayer.com. You can purchase my works and the works of other authors at **www.grayerpublishing.com**. That's my son.

Let me take time here to thank my family as a whole, who continually inspire me with their love and concern. To the many people willing to physically give a part of themselves is extraordinary. Special thanks to J.G. for your willingness to care for me when my illness was in control and for testing to go that extra mile. Thanks to A.G.; it looks like you're the one who will provide me the thing that will allow me to continue a normal lifestyle. Thanks to D.W. and J.W. for love and your assurance that you are there when needed and for your contribution to this work. By the way, you're looking good. Thanks S.G. and L.G. for being there when ever needed, whether called on or not; you guys are great. Thanks to my wife for all she does as we continue our journey through life; I love you. "I love you all."

From the Author

"This is a love story; it's not your typical love story but a love story nevertheless." That was part of a line from my first novel, *The Family Grant*. It was apropos to that story as it is to this one. There are consequences to every action, and love, or something akin to love, causes lots of consequences. Thus the title of my second novel, *If You Play, You Must Pay*. We see that in the lives of the people we meet in this story.

"Sometimes life is cruel, but there are times when it seems worse than that." "He thought of the permanency of death, and suddenly he realized that he didn't want to die." We don't know how we're going to respond to challenges that life hurls at us. Some of us are destined for doom because life is too hard, or we are too weak, but some of us are made stronger by life's challenges, which lead us to untold heights.

The journey of the Grant family continues, as Andrew's life is chronicled. Andrew is often in the doghouse during his journey. "The fact that he deserved to be in Joan's doghouse didn't make being there any easier." Sometimes people are caused to journey down roads previously never considered. "A woman can do all the things to another woman that a man can except get her pregnant."

The parallels from one generation to next are obvious. Andrew, like his father had a number of women and lots of children. There were big differences too. When Andrew brings a hooker home to parade in front of his children and their mother, something Luke would never have done. Luke has to step in. His action served as chastisement to his grown son, who was hurting at the time, but he was wrong too.

"I'm your father no matter what DNA tests say." When we think of one's contribution to the world we often look at their children, or to the children that they raise as theirs. "As he talked about the women in his life, you could see tears well in his eyes, but when he talked about the children whom he and those women produced, you could see a glow in those eyes." A person can't give anything more important to the world than worthwhile human beings to continue connections. Andrew contributed his share, as his children will contribute their share.

Also By Luther C. Grayer

The Family Grant

Chapter One

If You Play, You Must Pay
More Family Grant Connections

It was a Thursday evening, and Dr. Andrew Grant was finishing the installation of a crown on a patient's lower left molar. As the patient was rinsing, Dr. Grant's mind carried him back in time. He recalled the time that he cheated on his wife, Joan, by having sex with Miriam.

Miriam looked so beautiful that day, as Andrew sat watching her struggle to reach a glass on a top shelf in her kitchen. The glass continued to be just out of her reach, but she continued her effort. Her reaching caused her dress to rise up her thighs which revealed her pink panties. Andrew watched relishing the sight. He didn't know if he was reluctant to offer Miriam a hand because he didn't want to terminate his view or whether he was afraid to get too close to what he saw.

Andrew did eventually offer Miriam help. As he took a position behind her, they stood so close that their bodies touched. Andrew was able to reach the glass that had been out of Miriam's reach, but the glass was no longer the goal. Miriam and Andrew responded to the feel of each other that day, and they made love on Miriam's sofa.

Luther C. Grayer

Andrew's thought returned to the present when his patient said, "I'm finished, Doc."

Andrew took the paper cup from the patent and threw it in the trash.

After Andrew had finished with his patient, he was joined by his wife, Dr. Joan Grant. She was done for the day, since her 6:30 patient had canceled. Joan was glad the workday was over. Actually, their workweek was over since they only worked four days a week. The two doctors, along with a third partner, ran a successful dental practice in Chicago. In the winter, to escape the harsh weather of the Windy City, they traveled to their condo in sunny Arizona where they indulged in two days of golf and other recreation.

As the two doctors shared a light kiss to begin their long weekend, the receptionist announced that their son, A.J., was on line one. Joan took the call. A.J. was calling from the University of Arizona where he was a student. The initials A.J. were short for Andrew Jr. A.J. was twenty-three and the oldest child of Andrew and Joan. He was in his last year at the university and planned to teach high school after receiving his Master's degree in Education. He has always wanted to teach.

A.J.'s call caused Andrew to think about how close A.J. and his mother were and to remember how different it was in the beginning. Joan was a senior in high school when Andrew schemed and succeeded at getting her pregnant. She was a top student, with offers to several colleges, and she intended to pursue a fulfilling career. Getting her pregnant was Andrew's way of keeping her; that's when he put holes in his condoms and allowed his sperm to do its thing.

More Family Grant Connections

Joan was angry when she accidentally learned what he had done. From that point, until she forgave him, she made the rules, and she made Andrew pay. The rationing of sex was the hardest for Andrew, but he was willing to endure whatever punishment Joan deemed necessary.

Andrew's thoughts returned to the present when Joan said, "A.J. will talk to you tomorrow." The call caused Joan to remember how glad she had been when A.J. was finally born, as she felt freed from what felt like bondage. She remembered thinking that she wasn't going to let what Andrew had done stop her from getting the education and having the career that she wanted. She accepted an offer to attend Boston College and allowed Andrew to tag along. Her giving Andrew all the responsibilities for the care of their son were supposed to be his punishment, but it was really hers. Joan cringes even today when she remembers becoming detached from her baby as a punishment to his father. Joan's gradual or sudden realization of what she was doing to her son caused her to forgive Andrew, who, at worst, had given her a precious treasure.

Joan's thoughts returned to the present when Andrew said, "I can barely wait to get on the golf course.

This will be a four-day weekend since Monday is a holiday, and they were leaving Thursday instead of their usual Friday. Ann, the youngest daughter, and Eugene, the youngest son, were in Paris with their high school class. Andrew had talked to them last night which was morning in Paris. Ann and Eugene are scheduled to join the family Monday evening in Scottsdale.

Andy, Joan and Andrew's four-year old grandson, would sometimes travel with them, but he had a fever and wasn't able to travel this weekend.

Joan and Andrew had three hours to get to the airport for their flight. Joan suggested that they leave earlier for the airport so they could have a snack before their flight. She called the limousine service to see how soon they could be picked up. Their driver was there in ten minutes, knowing that his tip would be substantial for his effort.

On their way to the airport, Andrew's cell phone rang. It was their daughter Crystal, who, like her father, was a twin. Her brother, Christian, would be calling at any minute. They were a close family with the ages of the siblings being such that four of them were attending the University of Arizona. It was their choice to attend the same school. The fact that they chose Arizona was great. It allowed the family to get together often. Ann and Eugene were both in their last year of high school and would be starting college in the fall.

It's fortunate that Joan and Andrew are financially well off with the cost of raising a large family today. The couple earned well from their practice but would be well off even without it. Andrew was from a very wealthy family.

As predicted, Joan's cell phone rang before Andrew had finished his call with Crystal. It was Christian calling to check in. As they were nearing the airport, having ended their calls with the twins, they received a call from Austin, the sixth and last of the brood.

As they finished the call with Austin, Andrew had a flashback. Once again he saw Miriam struggling to reach a glass on the top shelf in her kitchen; that was the day that Austin was conceived.

Andrew's thoughts returned to the present when the driver opened the car door for him.

At the airport, Joan and Andrew finished their sandwiches when it was announced that their flight was boarding. When they reached their assigned seats, Andrew's fatigue was obvious; he managed to keep his eyes open just long enough for the plane to become airborne. Joan's day hadn't been as exhausting, so she was able to sit back and allow her mind to carry her back in time. She remembered the first time she met Miriam. It was during their college days before Miriam had gotten pregnant by Andrew.

Miriam was a teller at the bank and, even though Joan had seen her on campus, the two had never met. Joan was surprised to later learn that Miriam had been closer than she knew; she was roommate with Joan's best friend at school.

Joan still marveled at the fact that she liked Miriam right away and that they instantly became friends. Two months after she and Joan met, Miriam had gotten pregnant with Austin.

The day Joan learned of Miriam's pregnancy, the two women were having lunch on campus. At the time, Joan didn't know that it was Andrew's baby.

At lunch that day, Miriam, smiling broadly and gesturing in a manner that said look at me, asked enthusiastically, "Do I look different?"

Joan guessed instantly that Miriam was pregnant. She and Miriam were approaching best friend status despite the fact that they had only known each other for two months. Joan knew that Miriam and her boyfriend, Morris, had been trying to make a baby for weeks. Miriam wanted a baby badly, even though she and Morris weren't married and seemingly had no intentions of getting married.

As they finished lunch that day, Miriam playfully told Joan to pick up the pace knowing that she, too, wanted to get pregnant again. Miriam said, as a good friend might, "Let's keep my news our secret until you get pregnant too. It'll be great! We can be pregnant together."

Joan laughed to herself when she remembered how often she and Andrew had done it back then to get her pregnant. When Joan did get pregnant, the bond of sisterhood between her and Miriam grew even stronger. They were fulfilling the special charge of bringing forth the next generation.

Joan's thoughts returned to the present when the plane landed in Arizona.

There was a limousine waiting to transport Joan and Andrew to their condo. When they arrived at the condo, they found things perfect. Space age technology of 2013 was most apparent. Computers were so much more advanced now than they were seven years ago. Before leaving Chicago, Andrew had conveyed instructions via computer to their fully automated condo. After a two-hour flight from their office, Joan and Andrew arrived at their destination to find, as ordered, the lighting and the temperature of their bed and champaign perfect!

Andrew didn't need any of the aforementioned amenities to get in the mood for love. Even though his workday had been

More Family Grant Connections

strenuous, Andrew was now ready to make love to his wife. Standing next to Joan caused him sexual excitement. This woman had given him three children. She was the woman whom he had loved from the moment he first saw her and had determined then that she was the woman he would marry.

Joan and Andrew made love, and Andrew awoke the next morning renewed. He lay in bed while Joan showered in preparation for their golf round with friends. When Joan entered the bedroom wrapped in a white towel, parts of her body still wet.

Andrew said lustfully, "You look good, baby."

Joan, recognizing the tone, would normally entertain Andrew, but that would lead to other things and they had a tee time. Instead of performing for her husband, Joan dried quickly while encouraging him to shower. "The Thompsons are waiting," Joan said.

Joan and Andrew had missed many tee times in the past.

"Okay, baby, anything you say," said Andrew while thinking in silence *I'll get you later.*

After their round of golf, Andrew had to go to the bank. It was one of those rare instances, requiring his actual presence rather than a usual online communication. As Andrew and Joan stood in line waiting for the next available bank teller, Andrew's thoughts carried him back in time. He thought of the first time he met Miriam.

That day, Andrew and A.J. were in the bank to cash a check; Andrew was having trouble with his cranky one-year-old. Miriam, who was at the bank to apply for a job offered a helping hand. Her soothing voice and gentle touch quieted A.J. instantly. Miriam had a similar affect on Andrew. It was as if she was beckoning him.

Miriam was only a part-time student then taking one or two classes. Joan, on the other hand, was a full-time student who didn't spend much time with either Andrew or A.J. Joan's heavy school load wasn't the reason for the lack of time afforded Andrew. He was in her doghouse for getting her pregnant. The fact that Andrew deserved to be in Joan's doghouse didn't make being there any easier. It had been more than a month since Andrew had gotten some honey. Back then, it was part of his punishment that he and Joan only made love at Joan's behest, which wasn't often.

As Joan and Andrew continued their slow trek to the teller's window, Andrew recalled that after Miriam got the job at the bank, he would see her often, as he and A.J. did the family banking. Andrew would even create reasons to go to the bank in hopes of seeing Miriam. Finally, a mental connection was made and, even though Andrew was consumed with guilt, the pleasure was a kind of splendor that he couldn't deny himself. The fact that there might be a price to pay was not enough to dissuade him from continuing towards the bounty that lay ahead.

Andrew's thoughts returned to the present when Joan said, "Things are really moving slow," as they continued towards the bank teller. Joan nudged Andrew forward, as his mind had drifted. She said, "The teller is finally ready for you."

After finishing at the bank, Joan and Andrew headed home. As Joan drove through the mountainous terrain of Scottsdale,

More Family Grant Connections

Andrew couldn't resist touching her thighs as they loomed so prominently below the stylish outfit she wore.

In a tone indicating her arousal, Joan said, "You'd better wait until we get home unless you want us to run off this mountain."

Joan's comment caused Andrew to stop his probing short of the target allowing Joan to concentrate on the road. When they did pull into the driveway, Andrew knew that sex would still have to wait. Austin's car was in the driveway; an indication that he was home.

Austin, who was on the phone, hastily ended his call as Joan and Andrew entered the room. He moved towards them reaching Joan first. He hugged her tightly refusing to let go for a few seconds, and, then, he planted a juicy kiss on her cheek. He was known for his juicy kisses. Austin then greeted his father with a similar hug but spared him the kiss.

After a few minutes of conversation, Andrew excused himself and went to shower. As he showered, his thoughts carried him back in time; he recalled that one time that he cheated on Joan:

It was a Friday. Andrew had missed Miriam, whose workday at the teller window had ended before he and A.J. got to the bank. He was disappointed, for Miriam had become his source of mental fulfillment in the absence of actual physical affection. As Andrew and his son were leaving the bank, there stood Miriam at the door. It was as if she was waiting for them. Andrew walked Miriam home that day and they had sex on her sofa while A.J. was asleep in her bed.

Andrew broke off his affair with Miriam after they had sex. The sex was great but Andrew's feeling of guilt was greater.

It took all his strength to turn away from Miriam's beautiful body. He had succumbed to temptation that one time and was determined not to fall victim again.

Andrew's thoughts returned to the present when Joan entered the bathroom and jokingly asked, "Are you a prune yet?" He had been in the shower for a long time.

Andrew opened the shower door and said, "I'm glad you're concerned. I don't know about a prune but it has gotten rather puny. Come firm it up." Joan responded to Andrew's request and joined him in the shower. Things firmed up considerably.

After their romp in the shower, they adjourned to the bedroom. Joan fell asleep as soon as her head assumed a comfortable position on Andrew's chest. Andrew's thoughts carried him back in time; he thought of how it was when he and Joan were first married:

In the beginning, Andrew, and his new bride moved in with Andrew's parents; the house was large enough for two families. The plan was for Andrew and Joan to live there until Joan graduated high school. She had a year to go, which would be about ten months after the birth of her baby. Andrew completed his last year of high school and decided to work instead of starting college. He wanted to be available to help Joan through the pregnancy and her last year of school.

At the beginning of their marriage, things were good between Joan and Andrew. Sex got better and better each time they made love, and they made love a lot. Andrew's mother accepted his situation but harbored thoughts that her son had been tricked into his current situation. She thought Joan had deliberately gotten pregnant so that Andrew would marry her. Of course, just the opposite was true. Andrew had conspired to get Joan pregnant so that she would marry him.

One day, when he thought they were alone, Andrew told his mother the truth about Joan's pregnancy. He hoped his confession would give him relief from the guilt he felt for what he had done. Andrew didn't realize how far his confession had extended. Joan overheard the conversation

With tears rolling down her cheeks, Joan expressed how wrong it was for Andrew to conspire to impregnate her on purpose, even under the guise of love. She felt hurt and betrayed, and at that moment she determined to make Andrew pay.

Joan accepted the fact that she needed Andrew's help to get through her pregnancy and the next year of school. She needed his help, but it was going to be on her terms and once she had the baby, she would decide what to do next.

Andrew's thoughts retuned to the present when Joan snuggles next to him. He too fell asleep shortly after that.

The next morning, as Joan and Andrew were having breakfast, Austin came in. He had been out all night.

"Join us," said Joan.

Austin hugged Joan and greeted his father. "No thanks," he declared, and continued on to his room for sleep.

Seeing Austin caused Joan to recall when Miriam confessed that she had targeted Andrew to be the father of her baby. Joan remembered thinking at that time *this bitch seduced my husband while pretending to be my friend.* The truth was that Miriam had chosen Andrew before meeting him or Joan. She had overheard conversations between Joan and Debra and learned of Joan's marital problems. She knew before seeing Andrew that he was vulnerable. He needed female affection and Miriam wanted active sperms from an eligible donor. Andrew sounded like a perfect candidate for her to make a baby with. He would produce a child that would contribute something positive to the world.

Miriam had already sent her boyfriend, Morris, packing after learning that he knew that he couldn't make a baby but had led her to believe that there was something wrong with her. Miriam should have been suspicious from the beginning about the ability of a man with the name Morris Minor.

During Miriam's pregnancy, Joan felt something akin to sympathy for Miriam when, in a sad tone, Miriam said, "All the good ones are taken," indicating the lack of single black men who qualify as good candidates for fatherhood. Joan got the impression that, despite Miriam's young age, she had run into lots of losers. Joan had listened as Miriam expressed her radical philosophy. However, if Miriam thought that would square things between them, she was wrong.

The sound of the phone returned Joan's thoughts to the present. It was Andrew's twin sister, Angela, calling from Chicago.

As Andrew talked to Angela, Joan's thoughts carried her back in time, and she remembered Angela telling her the amazing story of her mother, Ann. Ann had intentionally gotten pregnant before she and Luke were married. She had planned to get pregnant without Luke's input. Joan had to laugh to herself as she thought that the phrase *without his input* was definitely the wrong choice of words. Luke had lots of input. He just didn't know at the time that that input was for him to make a baby.

More Family Grant Connections

The fact that people did devious things for the sake of love helped Joan to forgive Andrew for doing it to her, but she was ready to leave him when she learned that he had cheated on her and made a baby with Miriam. It was Angela who convinced Joan to stay, at least until she had her baby. They didn't know at the time that she was carrying twins.

Joan agreed that she could always leave after she had the baby. But, for now, she would share Andrew, who was so proficient at getting women pregnant. Joan was going to give him what every man seemed to want, but his two women might be hard to live with in their present conditions.

Joan's thoughts returned to the present when Andrew said, "Your turn," as he gave her the phone along with a kiss.

Joan talked to Angela; Joan also talked to her brother, Walter, who was married to Angela. Walter was still grieving heavily at the loss of their younger brother, Richard, who died six months ago. Walter couldn't get over thinking he should have done more to save his brother. Joan remembered Walter in Richard's apartment the day he was found dead. As they stood looking at their brother's lifeless body slumped against the refrigerator.

Walter said, "The last time I saw Richard, I gave him the money he asked for and watched him walk away. I accused him of being high on something, but he assured me that he wasn't."

The last time Walter saw his brother alive, he was either floating from some illegal drug that had been a part of his life for more than twenty of his thirty-seven years or he was being affected by the drugs that he now had to take for the numerous medical problems that he had. Whichever was the case, Walter never spoke to his brother again. Now he was forced to wonder if he could have done more to help him.

Joan, sensing the need that her brother needed to hear the words I love you, told him that she loved him.

She then said, "We should plan a party. We haven't had one since Richard's birthday three years ago." Walter told her that he loved her, too, and for an instant, he remembered how much of a party animal their brother was. Walter attended one of his brother's parties. Richard said it was to celebrate his new apartment, but it wasn't. It was just an excuse for a party. That's the way Richard was.

Wall-to-wall people were at Richard's party, looking as eloquent as any you would see anywhere. The women were gorgeous. It was on that night, when Walter walked into his brother's bedroom that he saw Richard in his element. Richard was stoned out of his head surrounded by more than a half dozen beautiful women, as if they were his protectors, shielding him from the world-at-large. If only they had been his protectors instead of patrons knowing where to score. Richard was connected and was his own best customers.

Walter's thoughts returned to the present when Joan said, "Andrew and I will pick you up tomorrow at the airport since I wasn't able to secure a limousine from the service." After the phone conversation, Joan and Andrew were off to play golf.

Playing golf was a part of Joan's healing from losing someone as close as a brother. She would beat the hell out of that little white ball.

Joan and Andrew were playing alone today. Their frequent playing companions had an emergency at home and couldn't make it. After the first nine holes, Joan waited in the cart while Andrew went to the clubhouse for refreshments. While waiting for her order, Joan's mind transported her back in time. She remembered how much she hated Miriam when she first learned that she had slept with Andrew and was claiming that she was pregnant with his baby. DNA tests later established that Andrew's one sexual encounter with the conspiring vixen had been sufficient to make a baby.

Joan's decision to share Andrew with Miriam, while they were both pregnant, was done both in a spirit of punishment and of necessity. She figured that catering to a woman at a time when she was at her neediest was work, at best. But, when multiplied by two, it had to be punishment. As far as necessity was concerned, there is a kind of sisterhood that exists between women that allowed Joan to feel sorry for her ex-friend, Miriam. Miriam was having a hard time due to the rumors that Morris had spread about her so she needed somebody's help to get through this.

Joan's thoughts returned to the present when Andrew returned with her sandwich and cold drink.

Andrew peeled the straw, careful not to touch the ends, and inserted it into the cup for Joan, before giving her the rest of her order. The gesture caused Joan to remember how diligent Andrew was during the early years in filling her every request when she and Miriam were pregnant with his babies. He did so regardless of how ridicules her requests were or how foul her disposition when she made them. Here's looking at those early years.

Chapter Two

The Early Years
Two Pregnant Women

Andrew was bone tired from the day's activities, but his work was nearly done. The only thing left to do was to put A.J. to bed. He was irritable from fighting sleep, trying hard to resist the Sandman. Andrew managed to soothe his son, which allowed him to fall asleep. Now finished with all his chores, and despite being tired, Andrew was looking forward to making love to his wife. When Andrew attempted to give Joan a kiss, she told him to go to Miriam tonight.

"I don't want Miriam tonight or any night."

"You did want her. You wanted her so much that you got her pregnant."

Andrew continued to protest, but not to the point that they argued. He didn't intend to cause Joan to leave him any sooner than she had already planned. Joan had made it clear that she would leave sooner if things didn't go exactly the way she wanted.

When Andrew arrived at Miriam's place, she had just awakened. She had on a long flannel robe that covered her completely, the kind of robe that a woman would never let a man that she was interested in see her wear. Andrew, with coldness in his voice, said, "Joan said that I should come here tonight."

Miriam hearing the coldness in his voice asked in a mocking but playful manner, "Baby mad at me? Well, you just join the crowd."

Andrew, with gritted teeth and clenched fists, did just that. "You are a conniving bitch, not worthy of being a mother, and I wish I could do something to prevent it."

Miriam, now angry too and ready for battle, said, "What makes you more worthy to be a father than me a mother? You only made a baby to keep a woman. I made one because I want a baby that contributes to the world." Miriam continued in a smart tone, "The only difference between you getting Joan pregnant and getting me pregnant is that in one case you were the screwer and in the other you were the screwee." Then, with even greater sass in her voice, she said, "I bet both of us felt good to you at the time."

Andrew couldn't help but laugh to himself at the truth of the classification. He had gotten screwed this time.

Miriam wasn't too angry with Andrew to ask him for help. Once again, she was struggling to reach something on a top shelf in the kitchen. She asked Andrew to get her the pork rinds that were too far back for her to get to. Andrew got the skins and gave them to Miriam. She tore open the bag and started to devour the contents. The way Miriam ate the skins prompted Andrew to ask what she had eaten for dinner.

Luther C. Grayer

Miriam said, "I must have slept through dinner."

Andrew with annoyance in his voice repeated, "Like I said before, you are not worthy of being a mother." He retrieved the partially eaten bag of skins and continued on to the kitchen saying, "You can have the rest of these after you eat some real food."

Andrew prepared a meal from the kitchen that he had stocked earlier in the week. A stocked kitchen evidently wasn't the problem, but preparing the food must have been. Andrew sat with Miriam while she ate; he even partook of the meal.

After eating, Miriam said that she was tired and went to bed. Andrew had become a proficient domestic worker since the birth of his son, and a good domestic worker never left dishes in the sink. As Andrew was finishing his kitchen duties, his cell phone rang. It was Joan professing a taste for carrot cake. She said, "If you're finished satisfying your woman, I really want a piece bad." Before Andrew could respond, Joan had hung up.

Joan's abrupt ending caused Andrew to remember two months ago when he confessed to her that he had slept with Miriam.

Andrew remembered that Joan had registered shock on two levels and he understood why when she said, "You know she's pregnant."

Andrew, in a startled manner as if he were talking to an ally, asked, "It's not my baby, is it?"

Indicating disbelief that she was being asked this question, Joan said, "I don't know Andrew. You should ask your woman. Or better yet, you might have it tested to know if it's your baby."

Two Pregnant Women

Andrew recognized his error. "You're right. What I meant was did she say whose baby it was?"

"Yes. She said it was Morris' baby."

"Who is Morris?"

Joan abruptly ended the conversation that night too; she said, "Go talk to your woman, Andrew. I have a headache."

Andrew's thoughts returned to the present when he finished with the last of the dishes. He called out to Miriam from the front door, as he was about to leave the apartment, but got no response. He went to the curtains that served as a partition separating the sleeping area from the rest of the apartment. When he parted the curtains, he saw Miriam in a fetal position in the middle of the bed. As Andrew moved closer, he could hear her sob and then he saw the tears streaming from her eyes.

Andrew, in a cold unconcerned manner asked, "What's wrong now?"

Miriam continued to cry, as she lay in bed. She said, "Things are such a mess, unlike when I first learned that I was pregnant. She blushed as she told Andrew how good he was at making love. She said, "Unlike Morris, you take your time with a woman. And, for sure, you don't shoot blanks." Miriam smiled when she said, "Too bad I didn't require more than one session."

Andrew, in a harsh tone said, "I don't see anything to laugh about. This is serious stuff."

"You're right." Miriam's smile vanished as she repeated again and again, "What a mess I made."

Luther C. Grayer

Andrew just sat hoping that Miriam would fall asleep so that he could leave. Miriam lay in bed allowing her thoughts carried her back in time. She replayed in her mind the conversation between her and Andrew two months ago when he first found out that she was pregnant:

Andrew said, "Joan told me you are pregnant."

Miriam registered genuine surprise that Joan had told what was supposed to be their secret, but she understood when she learned that Andrew had told Joan the bigger secret first. Miriam's jaws dropped when Andrew said, "I told Joan that we slept together."

Knowing that it was a lie, Miriam said, "Don't worry Andrew. It's not your baby."

"How can you be sure?" Andrew asked.

"I was already pregnant when I had sex with you that one time."

Miriam remembered Andrew breathing a sigh of relief as he said, "We still should have the baby tested like Joan said so that nobody has trouble down the line."

Miriam responded, "Sure, I can do that. I can do anything you want after my baby is born.

A few days later, Morris changed the picture. He told all of Miriam's friends that it wasn't his baby, as they were assuming. He even told Miriam's boss that it was her husband's baby creating problems for Miriam at work. Miriam had to quit her job after two of her girlfriends, on separate occasions, created a scene at the bank when they asked her if she was pregnant by their husbands. Morris had told them separately that Miriam was pregnant with their husbands' baby. Miriam didn't have any friends after Morris' rumors spread.

After Miriam had replayed past events in her mind she could barely keep her eyes open. As she was falling asleep, she said, "I should have left Boston and had my baby somewhere else."

Seeing that Miriam had finally fallen asleep, Andrew responded, "I wish you had left before I met you." He then left the apartment.

It was 2:30 in the morning when Andrew got to the all-night market. His only concern was that they not be out of that damn carrot cake. Andrew breathed a sigh of relief when he spotted what looked like two carrot cakes left on a middle shelf. But, as he drew closer, he could see that at least one of the cakes wasn't carrot. Andrew cursed under his breath and wondered where he was going to find a carrot cake at that time of morning. He was in luck. The second cake was carrot, but another customer reached it before he did and, for a split second, deliberated over which cake to take. The customer took the other cake causing Andrew to breathe another sigh of relief. He had his cake.

When Andrew returned home, Joan was asleep. He didn't know whether to wake her or not. Before he could decide, he heard her say, "Just a small piece with apple juice." Andrew was momentary panic struck as he tried to remember if there was apple juice in the fridge. At about the same time Andrew discovered that there was no apple juice, Joan's order changed. She said, "I want something tart, I want cranberry juice instead." For a second time that night, Andrew was fortunate. There was cranberry juice. Andrew served Joan her cake and juice. He knew she had had a good dinner. He served her that earlier.

After Joan had eaten, it was obvious to Andrew that she wanted something else. Andrew figured it was meant to be punishment since she had already sent him to another woman earlier that night. Andrew thought to himself that if Joan was trying to punish him by making him have too much sex, then bring it on. The truth was that making love with Joan could never be a punishment for Andrew. He loved her too much for that. This was one of those times, though, that they had sex but didn't make love. Joan didn't let that happen.

Andrew didn't awake until 7:30 the next morning, which was reasonable if his duties didn't start at 6:30 when his son awoke ready to eat. Joan and A.J. were at the kitchen table finishing breakfast. Andrew just watched them as they communicated by sounds, gestures and touches. He recognized something quite special between mother and child. And, for just an instant, he felt a twinge of envy knowing that a father's relationship would never equal it. When Andrew got to the table, he tried to plant a kiss on Joan's lips, but due to a slight turn of the head, at just the right moment, the kiss landed on Joan's cheek as per her intentions. The result was the opposite when Andrew attempted to kiss a clean spot on his son's cheek. A sudden turn of A.J.'s head caused their lips to make contact and Andrew got some of his son's breakfast.

Andrew was in for another busy day. Both Joan and A.J. had doctor's appointments. Andrew told Joan that Miriam hadn't eaten dinner last night when he'd gotten to her place.

Two Pregnant Women

Joan replied with indifference, "I'm sure you fed her, didn't you?" Andrew said that he would hire somebody to cook for Miriam. But, until then, he should check to see that she was eating properly.

Andrew asked, "Should I take A.J. with me now and come back for you later?"

Joan said in a somber tone, "No, I don't ever want my son in your woman's house."

It must have been the way Andrew reacted that made Joan ask, "A.J. has never been in her house, has he?"

Andrew started to say no, but how could he lie about a little thing like that after telling the truth about something as big as adultery. It was too late anyway. When Andrew didn't respond *"No"* immediately, Joan knew that the answer was yes.

Joan started to cry. "How could you have sex with your woman with my baby there?" Andrew now understood that you don't try to explain that A.J. was asleep in Miriam's bed while he and Miriam were having sex on the sofa. The only thing for him to say was that he was sorry and he will never do anything to hurt her again. Andrew left but promised to be back before ten so that he could fix lunch before they had to leave for their appointments.

When Andrew arrived at Miriam's place, the building was a mess from the construction work being done. Miriam answered the door in the same flannel robe that she was wearing last night.

"Welcome to hell. They started working at six this morning," Miriam said.

Andrew didn't respond to Miriam's reference to being in hell. He asked, in a gruff manner, "Did you eat breakfast yet?"

Miriam, in an equally gruff manner responded, "No, I didn't get hungry yet." Andrew continued onto the kitchen area and started breakfast. He wanted to get back home to Joan and A.J. While Miriam ate, Andrew did a little housekeeping. The inside of the apartment was as much of a mess as the outside. It was quite different from the first time Andrew saw it. In a stack of papers on a table in the living room, Andrew found Miriam's appointment schedule and saw that she had a doctor's appointment in thirty minutes. Andrew, with anger in his voice said, "Damn, Miriam, you should be at the doctor's office now."

Miriam said with surprise, "Is that today?"

Andrew, with even greater anger said, "Damn you, girl, what the hell are you doing? Are you trying to lose this baby?" Miriam, having matched Andrew's tone until now, didn't answer this time. Andrew, not getting some smart answer that he expected, repeated himself with even greater force. Miriam still didn't answer, but she did respond. Andrew could see tears streaming from her eyes. With no anger in his voice now, Andrew asked, "What's wrong with you?" Realizing no answer was coming, Andrew said, in an appeasing manner, "We can still make the appointment. You go get dressed."

Andrew continued to straighten up the apartment while Miriam dressed. There was an instant when the slightly opened bathroom door afforded him a glimpse of Miriam's naked body. She was four months pregnant but looked good. Even though she was carrying his baby, Andrew felt that he should turn away. He felt

Two Pregnant Women

like a pervert looking at her lovely body without her permission. He didn't turn away though. Andrew's view was terminated when Miriam moved to another part of the bathroom.

Miriam exited the bathroom minutes later fully dressed with the exception of street shoes. She quickly found the right pair, and then in a pleasant tone, not heard lately, she said, "I'm ready."

Miriam and Andrew were twenty minutes late for the appointment, but that was okay, since they never called you at the time of your appointment anyway. While they waited for Miriam to be called, Andrew went to the hall and phoned home. He explained to Joan what had happened and that he would be home in time to get her and A.J. to their appointments, if they eat before he gets there. Andrew said that he had planned to fix the fish that he had taken out of the freezer. He apologized because he wouldn't be there in time to fix lunch but promised to schedule time better from now on.

Joan sarcastically asked, "What are you fixing your woman for lunch?"

Andrew, not knowing how to answer just said, in a tired voice, "I don't know yet." He then ended the call saying he would be home in a couple of hours. Miriam's name was being called as Andrew was returning to his seat.

Miriam asked Andrew, in a voice that no man would have been able to refuse, "Will you come in with me?"

In the examination room, Miriam introduced Andrew to the doctor and the nurse as the father of her baby. Andrew and the doctor shook hands and participated in small talk while Miriam undressed behind the screen. The doctor left the room, and Andrew thought to himself, *what am I doing here? I hardly know this woman.* Then as if suddenly made aware of the fact that this woman was having his baby, it was clear why he was there. After getting Miriam's weight, the nurse directed her to the examination table with stirrups in place. The nurse adjusted the stirrups for Miriam's height and had her try them for fit before the doctor came in. After determining that the adjustment was correct, Miriam was allowed to lower her legs until the doctor was ready.

Andrew had never witnessed an exam like this before. It caused him to blush and that caused Miriam to ask jokingly, "Are you all right, babe?"

After the exam was finished and Miriam had dressed, she was given a prescription and a diet sheet and told that she had to eat better and get plenty of rest. Miriam wasn't gaining enough weight. The doctor also had the nurse change Miriam's appointment schedule so that she would be seen more often during the next two months.

On their way to Miriam's apartment, Andrew stopped at the pharmacy located in the supermarket. He put in Miriam's prescription but didn't wait until it was filled. He would pick it up tonight or tomorrow on his way back. Andrew did pick up some green beans to go with the pork chops and potatoes that he planned to fix for lunch.

When they reached the apartment, Andrew said, "You rest while I prepare lunch." He had almost two hours before he had to be home.

Two Pregnant Women

"Okay. I'll lie on the sofa." She could see Andrew as he prepared lunch. He was a good-looking man who was beginning to cause things in her to stir.

It wasn't long before Andrew called Miriam to lunch. After a quick trip to the bathroom, Miriam took a seat at her little kitchen table while Andrew remained standing.

"Aren't you going to eat or am I a Guinea pig for your food experiment?"

"I might as well eat now instead of waiting until I get home and have to heat something up." The food was good and Andrew was hungry. He hadn't eaten breakfast.

"What time is Joan's appointment?"

"1:30 and A.J.'s is at 3:00, but they are in the same building." Andrew told Miriam that he had fixed enough for her to have dinner if he didn't get back tonight. Miriam didn't respond. Andrew didn't pay it too much attention since he was running late and had to leave.

When Andrew returned home, Joan was sitting on the sofa, and A.J. was napping in his crib. Andrew tried, as he had earlier, to plant a kiss on Joan's lips. But this time his aim was so bad that he missed Joan completely. Of course, Joan's quick move had a lot to do with the miss.

As they drove to their appointments, Joan asked, "Did your woman make it to her appointment on time?"

"Yes, we made it." Andrew will have an occasion in the future to replay this question and answer in his mind, and he will realize that the best answer to the question would simply have been "yes."

Luther C. Grayer

"I'm glad you took time to call me while your woman was in the examination room."

Andrew was quick to correct Joan. Actually, he was too quick. "No, I called you before we went into the examination room." This was another reply that Andrew would come to realize should have simply been an acknowledgement of Joan's original statement. The best reply to the statement would have been, "I'm glad too."

With hoarseness in her voice, Joan replied, "You went into the examination room with her. You didn't go in with me."

Andrew was genuinely puzzled. "You wouldn't let me go in with you." Andrew has probably learned an important lesson from this small but revealing verbal exchange. The truth is just because a woman asks about another woman doesn't mean she wants to hear you talk about your relationship with another woman.

Joan's check up went well. She was in great shape with the two babies growing within her. Joan was more than two months pregnant, which meant that she had gotten pregnant as soon as she forgave Andrew and let him back in her bed full time. Joan was given a prescription to help lessen her bouts with morning sickness, which was the only problem she was having so far. Wanting a refresher course, Joan had asked for the name of a Lamaze instructor.

Now that the unborn babies had had their check up, it was time for A.J. In order to get to where A.J. was being seen, they had to use the crossover that connected two parts of the building divided by a street at ground level. A.J. insisted on walking and at fifteen months, it was a slow go. Despite A.J.'s protest, Andrew lifted him off his feet to speed up their travel.

Andrew's action prompted Joan to comment in a tone dripping with sarcasm, "Your daddy is in a hurry to get rid of you so he can get back to his woman." Andrew thought to himself that he had been father and mother to A.J. up until the time when Joan forgave him for getting her pregnant. She hadn't wanted much to do with him or A.J. until two months ago, and, now, she's saying that he's the one who wants to get rid of their son.

Andrew responded in a calm tone, while pointing to the clock on the wall. "It's 2:59."

Joan, looking at her watch, with a smidgen of "I'm sorry" in her voice said, "Oh, my watch has 2:30." They heard the nurse calling their name as they were turning the corner to the waiting area.

With a big sigh, Andrew said, "We made it." Then, he simply said, "I'll have the battery in your watch changed tomorrow."

Andrew now sat thinking as Joan appeased A.J. and the doctor did his work. Andrew was glad that he had responded as he had instead of as he felt. It would have been mean and unfair to insinuate that Joan wasn't a good mother. She was a good mother who had been angry with her baby's daddy.

Andrew's thoughts returned to the present when he heard A.J. cry, "Daddy." With outstretched arms, A.J. was trying to escape from what must now seem like an invasion by a monster in a white coat.

It was 4:30 when they returned home. After surveying what was on hand for dinner, Andrew decided on steak, rice and spinach.

Luther C. Grayer

Andrew prepared dinner while Joan entertained A.J. Andrew had the meal ready in forty minutes flat. He had to compliment himself remembering back two years ago when he could barely boil water. His mother had taught him a lot, and cooking was not minor.

After they had finished their meal, Joan asked, "Are you going to your woman's place now or later?"

"I should go now so that I can get back before A.J.'s bed time."

"Okay, maybe I can get a foot massage when you get back if you're up to it."

Andrew tried for a kiss on Joan's lips but got her cheek again. Andrew said, in a playful way, "I'll fix those feet up real good when I get back."

Andrew did hit his intended target as he placed a kiss on his son's lips, which were clean this time. Andrew told Joan that he would do the dishes later if she didn't feel like doing them.

On his way to Miriam's apartment, Andrew stopped at the pharmacy to pick up her prescription. When he arrived at Miriam's place, she wasn't in her flannel robe. She had on a short silk-like housecoat with a matching nightgown. Andrew continued on to the kitchen, not wanting to look directly at her for long. He remembered from grade school that, for fear of being blinded, you never look directly at something as powerful as the sun. At the moment, Miriam was smoking hot; looked as powerful as the sun.

Andrew asked, "Have you eaten yet?"

"No, I was waiting for you." She brushed past him and took a seat at the kitchen table.

Two Pregnant Women

"I'm going to fix your food, and you are going to eat. And then, I'm going home." Miriam teasingly asked, "We can't cuddle?" Then as she stood and tightened her sheer nightwear to conform to her body she asked, "Do I look fat?" Her sensual movements were interrupted by a knock at the door, which may have prevented an exhibition of Dirty Dancing 101. After locating and putting on her flannel robe, Miriam went to the door and asked, "Who's there?"

A familiar voice replied, "It's me, baby, open the door."

Miriam, instantly agitated, said in an angry tone, "Go away! I don't ever want to see you again."

"Come on, babe, open the door, I need to talk to you."

Miriam, now crying, said, "Go away, Morris, we have nothing to talk about." Morris angrily replied, "You open this door, or I'll kick it down."

Before Morris could act, if he intended to do so, Andrew, with matched anger warned, "Go away, Morris, or you're going to have a problem."

By then, Andrew had reached the door. He pushed Miriam aside but before he could say more, he heard footsteps. Morris conceded, obviously preferring not to confront an unexpected man. In an insulting way, Andrew asked Miriam, "Are you still sleeping with him?"

Miriam, with a toughness in her voice, replied, "Why do you care?" Before Andrew could respond, Miriam asked again, "Why do you care?" but with no toughness this time. "What do you care what I do?"

"I care because of this baby."

Luther C. Grayer

"Okay, Andrew, I do owe you an explanation. It's a long story."

"Then you'd better get started so that I can get home."

Andrew reheated Miriam's dinner as she talked. She continued to talk during and after her meal. As Miriam talked, anyone could tell that her background as a psychology major loomed heavily in her philosophy.

Miriam had concluded from her observations and personal experiences that her community was in trouble, lacking eligible black men to keep her community progressing in a world that was advancing in technology daily. Black men were in jails or on drugs in numbers that could create an inferior race of blacks, and we can't stand to be more inferior, as a group, than the white establishment has already caused. Miriam concluded that eligible black men had to be shared, so that we create a population able to continue to contribute its share to world progress.

Chapter Three

The Early Year
Changing Feelings

As Andrew washed the dishes, he marveled at Miriam's psychological analysis and where it placed him in the scheme of things. Andrew might be flattered. Even though he was thought of as stock in Miriam's world, he was considered prime stock. He was desired for procreation. For Andrew, the problem with Miriam's world was that the results, whatever they are, didn't come from love or some emotion akin to it. Upon greater consideration, Andrew had to revise that thought, at least in his case. Physical attraction was a powerful emotion that often leads to love. Andrew had been set up, but he had responded based on emotion. Miriam's body was a powerful stimulus.

Andrew was finishing the last of the dishes as his mind was ending its dissection of Miriam's philosophy. His thoughts returned to the moment when Miriam told him that she hadn't intended to cause a problem for him and Joan.

"I didn't even intend to tell either of you that it was your baby," Miriam said. "That is until Morris made it necessary. I would have told the child when he or she was old enough who his or her siblings were. I wouldn't want brothers and sisters to meet and have a romantic affair." Miriam's reference to A.J. as somebody's brother caused Andrew to realize it was well past his son's bedtime.

"I've got to go. Do you think Morris will come back?"

With a grin, she said, "No, he's gone at least for the night." She was being facetious since there were officially only three minutes before it was officially morning.

"Okay, you keep this door locked and I'll see you in a few hours." Then Andrew left.

When Andrew arrived home, A.J. and Joan were asleep. Andrew took a seat on the sofa for what was suppose to be a minute, but it wasn't long before he too was asleep. Andrew didn't awake until 7:39 that morning, and once again, he found Joan and A.J. at the kitchen table just finishing breakfast. A.J. reacted with enthusiasm when he saw Andrew. A.J.'s enthusiasm increased as Andrew drew closer and spoke to his son in their special language. Maybe a father can have as special relationship with their child as can a mother. Andrew kissed A.J. and turned to kiss Joan who turned and was out of her chair before Andrew could come close to making contact.

"You worked overtime last night," said Joan.

Andrew said, "Miriam told me her story. Why didn't you tell me that she set me up?"

"Are you saying she made you have sex with her?"

Andrew simply answered, "No." He realized that he couldn't win by telling of the mesmerizing affect that Miriam had on him at the time. Andrew did say, "I was wrong, but I was lonely."

Changing Feelings

Joan's next question came as a momentary surprise, but it had been anticipated. "Do you like sex with her more than with me?"

Andrew knew the answer to Joan's question had to be definite with no hesitation, and the answer he gave could go a long way towards getting her back. He answered with no equivocation in his voice. "Sex with nobody could ever be as good for me as it is with you." Andrew loved Joan and would never have a problem with that question under any condition.

As if tired of the conversation, A.J. threw part of his breakfast splattering his parents.

Joan responded to her son's call for attention. "You're right it is time for your bath."

As Joan left for the bathroom with A.J. in tow, Andrew asked, "You do know that I haven't had sex with her since that one time?"

Joan with no sign of favor or disfavor with Andrew's reveal just said, "No, I didn't know that." She added, "Don't take her to my Lamaze instructor." Andrew hadn't thought of a Lamaze class for Miriam until now.

As Andrew was leaving the apartment, he said, "I'll be back in two hours for sure this time."

As Andrew was getting out of his car in front of Miriam's apartment building, he saw Miriam struggling to free herself from the grasp of a man. Andrew had seen a snapshot of the man in Miriam's apartment. Andrew was moving with the speed of a greyhound. As he approached the struggling couple, he shouted, "Let her go!" The man did let go and took off running. Again, he obviously preferred not to confront Andrew. Andrew only gave chase for three or four strides before returning to see about Miriam. Andrew breathing heavier than normal asked, "Are you alright, did he hurt you?"

Miriam with coolness said, "I'm fine."

Andrew breathing normal now asked, while almost touching Miriam's stomach, "Should we go to the hospital?"

"No, let's go up stairs."

"What does he want?"

"Let's go upstairs," Miriam repeated. "I'll tell you then." They had to maneuver past piles of debris from the construction work going on. When they reached Miriam's apartment, Andrew asked if she'd had breakfast. Before Miriam could answer, Andrew asked what was she doing out so early?

"No I haven't eaten yet. The answer to your second question is you don't know me very well, Mr. Grant. Once I walked in the morning all the time. Morning is my favorite time of day, especially early morning."

"Do you want one egg or two?" And, in the same breath he asked, "What does Morris want? That was Morris wasn't it?"

Miriam in jest answered, "One, money and yes." Andrew did a double take. "If you are going to ask me three questions at once then I'm going to give three answers at once."

"Okay I understand the *one* egg and the *yes* that it was Morris, but tell me what you mean about *money*."

Miriam told Andrew that when Morris learned that he was a member of the wealthy Grant family he wanted me to blackmail your father. He figured he would pay to keep this a secret.

Changing Feelings

"I'll handle him when he comes back," Andrew declared.

"I don't think he'll be coming back. I told him that Mr. Grant knew about his expected grandchild, and that he was looking forward to welcoming it into the world. I made him aware of what could happen to an associate professor if he messes with a powerful man's family." Miriam then said, "Your timing was perfect. I had already told Morris that you would be here any minute, and when you jumped out of that car you should have seen his face."

"I did, I just don't know what it was saying."

Miriam's last words were, "He's gone and won't be back. He thinks things are good between us."

Andrew said, "Come eat your breakfast."

After they had finished eating, Miriam asked what time he had to leave. Andrew said he was going as soon as he did the dishes. Miriam told him that she would do the dishes later. She asked if he would do her a favor instead. Andrew was reluctant to say yes thinking it might be something sexual. He was ashamed that he had thought such a thing when Miriam asked him to play a couple of hands of bid whist.

"I'm not very good," said Andrew.

"That's okay; I want some company."

After just a few hands, it became obvious that Andrew was correct when he said he wasn't very good. Actually, it wasn't that Andrew was so bad. The truth was that Miriam was so good. When they quit Miriam was close to winning by going over the top and Andrew was close to losing by going out the backdoor.

"We'll finish this when I get back. For lunch, warm up what was left from yesterday, and I will be back before dinner time."

Luther C. Grayer

Miriam responded in a military manner while giving a salute, "Aye, Captain," but she added in a non-military way, "I'll be waiting."

When Andrew returned to Miriam's place, she was wearing her flannel robe again. Andrew was glad, since the outfit she had on last night was hard to take, or maybe it would be more correct to say it was not hard to take. The outfit was quite pleasing to the eye and the only reason for her to wear it was to cause that kind of reaction. Andrew didn't know why Miriam wanted to get him hot. Her baby was on the way, and in her scheme of things, he had served his purpose.

Andrew could smell the food that Miriam had prepared as soon as he entered the apartment. It smelled delicious, unlike anything he could cook. "What's that?" Andrew asked, having taken in a deep breath before and after his question.

Miriam named some dish that was obviously above Andrew's 101 cooking level. "Sit down, it's ready."

Andrew did what Miriam said. He allowed himself to be served even though he had already eaten at home. Andrew's first mouthful indicated that Miriam's skill level was that of a master chef.

After dinner, they finished their game of bid whist and Andrew was getting back into the game. He was getting out of the hole, but couldn't help but suspect that Miriam was letting him win. He figured, like cooking, her skill level at bid whist was master level as well.

After just a few hands into their second game, Andrew said, "I have to go. It's almost A.J.'s bedtime."

Changing Feelings

"Even A.J. doesn't go to bed at 6:00 o'clock in the day."

Andrew without responding to Miriam's comment said, "I have a woman coming tomorrow to cook and clean for you."

In a tone indicating irritation Miriam said, "I don't need a woman, I need a man."

Andrew matched Miriam's tone and said, "Do you want me to send a man instead?"

Dejectedly Miriam said, "Just go, I don't need you to send either, I do need some money though. I have some bills to pay."

"Write your account number, I'll put some money in your account tomorrow." Miriam wrote the number quickly and jammed the piece of paper into Andrew's shirt pocket. She then said with emphasis, "Now go and fuck your wife." Miriam continued with her vulgarity. "Oh, but that's what got your ass in trouble the first time isn't it? Your wife didn't want to fuck you, so you fucked me instead."

Andrew matching Miriam's force but not her vulgarity said, "I am not going to do that again, I am not going to let you."

Before Andrew could finish his statement, Miriam cut him off and said, "I didn't make you have sex with me, you saw what you wanted and you went for it."

Andrew didn't say anymore but he did think more. Miriam was right, he had seen what he wanted and now despite the mess he'd created, he still wanted it but he wanted his wife more. On his way out of the building, Andrew stumbled twice. He mumbled to himself, "This place is a death trap."

When Andrew returned home, Joan was on the floor playing with A.J.

47

Luther C. Grayer

"Look, A.J., your daddy is home and on time for a change."

Andrew could sense from Joan's greeting that there wasn't going to be any lovemaking at home tonight. Joan told Andrew that his father had called while he was out. "I started to tell him that you were at your woman's place, but I thought I would let you tell him that you cheated on me and A.J."

Before he gave adequate thought, Andrew replied, "I had to confess to somebody or I was—" Again, before Andrew could get out another word he realized he had made another mistake; he just didn't know what it was.

The tears streaming from Joan's eyes confirmed in Andrew's mind that it was a big mistake. "Baby, I'm sorry." And he was. He just didn't know what he had done. "What did I do this time Joan?"

Joan while drying her eyes said, "You told your father about your woman first. Did he tell you how to fix this mess? Did he tell you how he managed all the women in his life?" Joan now with attitude in her voice said, "You screwed me, giving me a baby and you run and tell your mama. You screwed me by giving your woman a baby and you run and tell your daddy. What's with you and this guilt thing anyway? You think you can do wrong and because you feel guilty, it makes everything all right. Did your mama and daddy tell you what to do? Do you handle any of your business yourself?" Joan now as if these were to be her last words said, "I want you to leave and not live here anymore."

Andrew refused to allow this to be the end. He figured he just had to beg harder. As serious as the moment was, Andrew couldn't help but laugh to himself when he thought of the lyrics

Changing Feelings

to a popular song that said *I ain't too proud to beg.* "I've done you wrong, baby, I know it, but let me make it up to you."

Joan continued to attend to A.J., giving no verbal response to Andrew's pleas. After more pleas from Andrew, Joan responded with tears. She said while still crying, "Can you take back your sex with Miriam?" Not allowing Andrew to answer Joan continued, "No you can't take it back." With fewer tears now, Joan said, "What do you see in her anyway?" Once again Andrew wasn't allowed to answer before Joan said, "Maybe I should see what sex is like with somebody else." Still not waiting for Andrew to comment, "Yeah, that's it, can I have sex with somebody else Andrew, since I've never had sex with anybody but you? Can I Andrew, will you still love me then?" Finally, Joan gave Andrew a chance to respond.

Andrew with tears in his eyes at the thought of Joan sleeping with another man said, "I'll always love you."

If Joan felt this should be his punishment, then so be it. If she wanted to see what it would be like to make love with another man, it was okay. He would be there when she finished. It was as he had said in his goodbye letter a year ago, *I know that when you finish, you'll realize that nobody could love you as much as I do.*

Then Joan asked, "Would you love me if I had sex with your woman?"

The question took Andrew by surprise. He wondered what was going on in Joan's mind. Was she becoming a lesbian or did she just want to do something to hurt him? Andrew didn't know what was happening, but he was afraid that he couldn't compete if his wife's sexual orientation had changed.

Joan's question was as much of a surprise to her as it was to Andrew. It caused her to question herself wondering if the instant connection she felt in the beginning for Miriam was still there, even after what she had done. Joan thought in silence, *why am I aiding and abetting this woman who slept with my husband?* Joan expressed amazement to herself when she realized that she had sent her husband to help Miriam.

Andrew responded to Joan's final question by simply repeating, "I'll always love you no matter what."

Joan's final statement was, "I don't want to do this anymore, Andrew. I want you to leave and not live here."

Chapter Four

The Early Years
Sexual Revelation

Andrew complied with Joan's request. He moved out of their apartment, but he refused to go far. He was not going to leave his son and his two unborn babies. Andrew took an apartment in the same building; the apartment was supposed to go to another couple, but Andrew offered to pay the landlord a year's rent in advance. Andrew moved Miriam into the apartment with him while construction work was going on in her building. Andrew had decided that he may have lost Joan, but he was going to take care of his children, and that meant taking care of Joan and Miriam, at least, until they had their babies.

Andrew was still busy, but it was easier than when Joan and Miriam lived on different sides of town. He could even get away with fixing lunch and dinner once a day, since he could serve the same meal to both women as he shuttled from one apartment to the other.

Luther C. Grayer

At this point, it was difficult to think of either Joan or Miriam as Andrew's woman, since neither of them was giving up anything remotely close to honey. For Andrew, things in the love department were zero. Two months ago, he and Joan were at least occasionally doing it, but now she had shut down completely. It was as if it was just yesterday that Andrew had violated her trust.

One evening, after having fed everyone, Andrew was playing bid whist with Miriam. He had gotten good enough to, on occasions, beat his superior opponent. Andrew asked Miriam point blank, "Why haven't you tried to seduce me since I moved you in here?"

"Because I don't want you."

Andrew, while assuming his version of a sexy feminine pose, said, "You wanted me just last week when you were still in your apartment and had on that sexy night gown."

Miriam responded in a way that a teacher might when trying to make a distinction between what was heard and what was meant. "I wanted you sexually. I didn't want to take you from your wife. Last week, you were still fighting to get her back, and you would have eventually succeeded, but you quit." Miriam made a special effort to emphasize the difference between her sharing him and her taking him.

Andrew showing frustration said, "First of all I didn't quit trying to get her back. I was put out of our apartment." Continuing to show frustration with up stretched arms, he said, "Two women are carrying my babies, and neither of them wants to sleep with me. Goodnight! I'm going to bed."

Sexual Revelation

Andrew's bed was the sofa, just as it had been most of the time in the other apartment. As he prepared his bed, the essence of Miriam's statement played in his head, *if you can't get your wife to give you some, then I'm not going to give you any either.*

It would be wishful thinking on Andrew's part to think that Joan was adversary to Miriam or vice versa, since neither of them had any interest in him now. Whatever classification was appropriate for these two women's relationship it wasn't working in Andrew's favor. Andrew fell asleep as soon as his head touched the pillow. He was drained from the day's activities and had to be up again at six in the morning for A.J.

Miriam was careful not to awaken Andrew as she left the apartment. When she got to Joan's apartment, she was almost ready to turn around and go back upstairs. Her knock at Joan's door was probably insufficient to be heard unless Joan was sitting at the door. Miriam forced herself to knock harder, knowing that she had deliberately knocked too soft the first time.

"What can I say?" Miriam asked herself aloud. "I've already told her why I did what I did. There's nothing else." But, Miriam knew there had to be something else she could say to make things better; she just didn't know what it was.

Miriam was about to leave when she heard the door opening and suddenly it was too late to turn back. Joan and Miriam's eyes met. Miriam asked if she could come in expecting the answer to be no. Joan, without speaking, opened the door wider and walked back into the apartment. Miriam followed Joan and saw A.J. playing in his crib. The crib sat in the middle of the room, and A.J. was enthralled with some task that was helping to develop his senses. Miriam, uncharacteristically, could have melted from Joan's piercing stare that seemed to penetrate her soul. Normally, it would take more than a look from a woman to affect Miriam that way. But, perhaps knowing that her actions had pierced her friend's heart made her feel differently.

Miriam asked, "Can I have a drink of water please?"

Joan, knowing how much she herself liked ice cold water lately responded, "Would you like ice in it?"

Miriam reacted, as if a glass of ice water at that moment was an elixir of the gods. "I would die for that," she said.

At that moment, the two women realized that being pregnant gave them knowledge of each other that they might otherwise not have. To know what one was feeling because somebody tells you was one thing, but to know what somebody was feeling because you had felt it too was something more. At that moment, the two women recognized in each other the importance of motherhood. They were carrying the next president, the next Einstein, or the person who might find the cure for the world's most vile disease. It was as if they now realized, they really did have a mission, an important mission, and at least they deserved each other's respect.

After preparing Miriam's ice water, Joan attended to A.J., who was now demanding attention. Joan told Miriam that her stretch cream was on the top shelf in the bathroom as she noticed that Miriam couldn't resist rubbing what appeared to be an itching belly.

"Thank goodness!" Miriam exclaimed, as she made her way to the bathroom to soothe what truly was an itching belly.

Sexual Revelation

When Miriam returned from the bathroom, Joan said, "You must have thought that I was crazy when Andrew told you what I said."

Miriam didn't know what Joan was talking about, but she went along since they were at least talking.

"Yes, well, we're all a little crazy." Miriam said.

Joan responded, "People shouldn't just let things happen to them. They should make things happen for them."

Miriam tried to think of some way to respond herself that would cause Joan to reveal what she was talking about. Miriam knew it had to do with what she and Andrew had done, but what does Joan want to do about it? Miriam decided to take a chance that Joan really was referring to the fact that she'd had sex with Andrew. She said to Joan, "You know that sex is only a physical thing, don't you?"

"Does that mean that it's alright to just do it if you want to try it?"

Miriam, hoping that this would serve as an apology, and would make what she did more acceptable, said, "Yes, if you didn't intend to hurt anybody. It's just a physical thing." Miriam was about to continue with her effort to apologize when Joan walked over and kissed her on the mouth.

Joan said, "Let's start tomorrow after I put A.J. to bed."

As Joan was leading A.J. to the bathroom for his bath, she said to Miriam, "Pull the door shut on her way out."

Miriam managed to make her way to the door without attempting to confirm what had just happened. On her way to her apartment Miriam asked herself if that had been her square and straight-lace friend who, she figured, had to have the lights out in the room when she had sex with her husband.

When Miriam returned to her apartment, Andrew was still asleep. She didn't wake him and had decided not to ask what Joan was talking about. Miriam figured if he was suppose to tell her something and he didn't, then he had his reason, so she would wait and let Joan tell her or, maybe, show her. Miriam then went to bed.

The next morning, Joan joined Andrew in the kitchen as he was preparing their son's breakfast. Joan gave Andrew a cordial greeting and asked what Miriam had said when she came back last night.

Andrew, looking puzzled as he asked, "When she came back from where?"

"From here." Joan said.

"What was she doing here?"

Now, Joan looked puzzled As she said, "I thought she came because of what you told her."

"I didn't tell her anything."

Before Joan could respond, Andrew said, "Are you talking about the sex thing? I thought you were kidding. You were kidding weren't you?"

Joan, with a slight grin, said, "Of course, I was kidding." Their focus was diverted when A.J.'s cry summoned his mother.

Andrew, now nearly finished preparing breakfast, asked, "Do you want me to get him?"

"No, you finish what you're doing. I'll have him ready for his breakfast in five minutes. That's not too soon is it?"

Sexual Revelation

"Not at all; breakfast will be ready in three minutes flat."

It had been another busy day, with Andrew living up to his obligations in a personal way. Operating out of both habit and a desire to stay connected, Andrew was taking care of what had become his family. He had been taking care of Joan and A.J. that way since A.J.'s conception. In the beginning, it had been one way to be around Joan more at a time when she didn't want much to do with him. It was, in part, the same today. But as always, there was a real sense of responsibility. Andrew was committed.

That night, Joan and Andrew stood looking down at A.J. after he'd finally succumbed to sleep. Andrew kissed Joan on the cheek and tried to continue on to her lips. Joan turned away, and said, "Not tonight, Andrew."

As Joan turned to walk away, Andrew grabbed her arm and pulled her back. "Please, Joan, I want you so much."

Joan, while attempting to free her arm said again, "No, not tonight Andrew."

Andrew didn't let go of Joan's arm, prompting her to ask, "Are you going to make me, Andrew? Are you going to make me do this?"

"You're my wife, Joan, and I want you."

"Does that mean that you can make me do this, Andrew?"

At that moment, A.J. awoke and bellowed as if he were defending his mother. Andrew let go of Joan's arm as if responding to the charging hero. Joan went to her son, as if she wanted to thank him for saving her.

The next day, while Andrew and A.J. were out doing errands, Miriam paid Joan another visit. This time Miriam's first knock was loud enough for Joan to hear. Joan opened the door. She asked, "What do you want, Miriam?"

Miriam apologized for not coming last night, saying she thought it was best not to come since Andrew seemed upset when he returned to their apartment.

Miriam asked, "What happened between you guys last night anyway?" Miriam sensing that no answer was coming didn't bother to persist but went to something of more concern to her. She asked, "What was the kiss for last night?"

Miriam could see that Joan was uncomfortable with the question, but she didn't let that stop her from pursuing the matter. Moving towards Joan, Miriam asked the question again. When Miriam got close enough, she kissed Joan lightly on the lips but applied more pressure when she kissed her a second time. Miriam parted Joan's lips with hers so that their tongues could touch. Their kiss was interrupted when they heard Andrew's key enter the front door lock. Joan and Miriam had enough time to part themselves before Andrew entered the apartment

Andrew, with a sleeping A.J. and other packages in his arms registered surprise when he saw Miriam there. He continued on to A.J.'s room and unloaded his cargo. He put his son in his bed and affectionately tucked him in. When Andrew returned from A.J.'s room, Joan and Miriam were sitting at the kitchen table. Before Andrew could join them, the phone rang. It was Victoria, Andrew's father's second wife; she was calling from Chicago.

Victoria gave Andrew some real bad news. There had been

an auto accident. Andrew's mother was killed and his father was in coma.

Andrew was distraught at the news; only after he talked to his sister later that evening did he gain enough composure to book passage on the first flight available for him and A.J. Joan wanted to go, but she couldn't fly when pregnant; it made her sick. She would take the train later.

Joan and Miriam went to the airport with Andrew and A.J. Miriam gave Andrew a hug and said, "I'm sorry. I will pray for your father."

Joan with tears in her eyes, said, "Call me as soon as you get there. Kiss Luke for me, and even if he's not awake, tell him that I love him." Joan then hugged both A.J. and Andrew while A.J. was in his father's arms.

Andrew said, while looking at the two women, "Take care of each other and our babies while I'm gone." He then turned and walked through the boarding doors.

It was 11:20 that night when Andrew's plane landed in Chicago. He was met at the airport by his sister, Angela, who couldn't stop kissing her nephew whom she hadn't seen for months. Angela drove them home so they could put A.J. to bed. It was well past his bedtime, and he was worn out. Angela had Andrew to move A.J.'s crib into her room. She kept her nephew while Andrew went to the hospital to see their father.

When Andrew entered his father's room, he saw Victoria asleep in the chair next to his bed. Victoria had been like a godmother to Andrew and his sister when they were kids. She has had a special relationship with his parents for as long as Andrew could remember.

Luther C. Grayer

Victoria awoke when Andrew touched her on the shoulder. She started to cry. "Our Ann is gone. Oh, Andrew! Our Ann is gone."

They cried while embracing, and Andrew remembered once having seen Victoria and his mother share a light kiss as two good friends might do in celebration of some event. Victoria, with great sadness in her voice said, "I can't lose Luke too."

Victoria's gloom caused Andrew to recall the first few lines of a poem:
> Her sadness was so total that it permeated the room and made it unsafe for others. Her knower wanted to cut out the pain, and end the sadness, but knew not what tool to use.

At that moment, Andrew realized that Victoria still loved his father, who'd had two other wives since her.

Suddenly, as if she hadn't finished her first statement, Victoria said, "But he's going to be alright. Luke is going to be alright."

After talking to the nurse, Andrew called Joan. He told her that Luke was holding his own and all they could do was wait for him to wake up. "We're going to wait as long as possible before having mother's funeral, so there's plenty of time before you need to come." Andrew asked how she and Miriam were doing.

"We're fine, but don't worry about us. Do you want to speak to Miriam? She's here."

Andrew said, "No," and then he declared to Joan his unconditional love. Andrew ended the call saying, "Do whatever you need to do to be able to accept my love again, for I'll always love you."

Sexual Revelation

After Andrew's call, Miriam asked, "What did you say to Andrew?"

"You're sitting right here. You heard everything I said."

"You know that I'm talking about the other night." Miriam asked again. "What did you tell him the other night?"

Joan, thinking in silence, recalled the first time she saw Miriam, and how much she liked her right away *Did I want to have sex with her then? Did I see the same thing that Andrew saw; a beautiful woman who turned me on?*

Joan's thoughts returned to the moment when she felt Miriam's hand on her shoulder. Sensing that Miriam was about to speak, Joan told her that she had asked Andrew if she could have sex with his woman. "That's what I said to Andrew that night."

Miriam responded with surprise. "You called me his woman? We only had sex that one time, and I don't think I would have had a chance if he had been getting it at home." Miriam asked curiously, "What did Andrew say? Did he give you permission to have sex with me?"

"He sure did, but he thought that I was kidding when I asked."

"Were you kidding, or do you really want to have sex with me?" Miriam asked.

Joan said, "This is crazy. I bet you would never have thought of something like that."

"Maybe not, but I've never been one to pass on a good idea just because I didn't think of it." Miriam then kissed Joan and caressed her breast. "Are yours tender?"

"No," she said as she enjoyed the feel of Miriam's touch.

Luther C. Grayer

They continued to explore each other's bodies as if they were unfamiliar with the female form. What was this pantheon that was always so close, yet never recognized for its true magnificence? They marveled at each other's middle as they caressed, and they laughed when they listened to each other's inner workings. A touch of their jewel sent pleasure through their bodies at least equal to the best they had ever felt.

Joan and Miriam made love that night, like two kids without a care in the world. For the next few days, while home alone, they went out and experienced the world during the day, and at night, they stayed in and experienced each other. One day, while they were out, Morris, while with a couple of his friends, witnessed Joan and Miriam's inability to resist sharing a kiss. Morris, in a taunting manner, called Miriam a whore who screwed men and kissed women. He caused a scene and wouldn't stop until Joan, in a most un-lady like way said, "Go away, little dick, before I cut it off and shove it down your throat."

Morris, stunned and seemingly embarrassed that some secret had been exposed, walked away unable to respond.

Miriam, shocked as well, said, "Where did that come from? And how did you know about the little —"

Before Miriam could finish her question, Joan burst out laughing and said, "You mean." Miriam was now laughing too, while nodding her head and spreading her two index fingers an inch apart to indicate the size of the aforementioned body part.

When the two women got home, they parted long enough to agree that Andrew was the only "Man" that should contain the fire burning in them. He was the father of the babies whom they were carrying so his should be the only fireman on duty until those babies are born. They would get through the rest of their pregnancy by sharing Andrew in a way that they hadn't up until now. The two women agreed that they were both in need of his services even after finding each other. The fact that Miriam had been without Andrew's services longest gave her dibs. Joan convinced her to come to Chicago with her for Ann's funeral.

Their train ride was like a holiday. And, even though they were going for a solemn occasion, it was a festive experience. The two women enjoyed the trip. When they got to Chicago, they stayed in the house that Andrew and his sister grew up in. Joan and Andrew had lived there when they first got married two years ago. They lived in the section of the house that was originally called Victoria's wing. It was a two-bedroom apartment and was called Victoria's wing because it was built for Luke's second wife, Victoria. She lived there while Andrew, Angela, and their parents lived in the main part of the huge house.

It was a big house for sure, and there had always been lots of people in and out when Andrew was growing up. It was like the old days again. There were lots of people in and out of the house. Joan and Miriam shared a bedroom, and Andrew took the other bedroom in Victoria's wing. Angela continued to keep her nephew in the main part of the house; she would be returning to school soon and wouldn't see him again for a while.

Luke's other daughter and her husband, and Luke's other son also stayed in the house while in town for Ann's funeral. Luke's other three children who lived in Chicago were also in and out of the house a lot during this time.

Chapter Five

The Early Years
Lifestyle Change

It was Joan and Miriam's second night in Chicago. Joan heard Andrew as he returned home from visiting his father; she had been waiting for him. Joan followed Andrew into his bedroom.

"How is Luke doing?" Joan asked

Andrew, in a positive tone, said, "His breathing is stronger. They say that's a good sign."

Joan felt from what Andrew said, and from how he sounded, that he was all right for sex. In fact, it might be just what was needed since, as far as she knew, he hadn't had any for a while. Joan stroked Andrew's thigh as he sat on the side of his bed. Andrew's manhood was quick to attention.

Joan then leaned forward and whispered in Andrew's ear, "Come with me."

At that moment, Andrew could have been led off a cliff. He followed Joan back to her room where Miriam was asleep. Joan, holding Andrew's hand, led him to the side of the bed. Without

Lifestyle Change

speaking, she let go of his hand and, with Andrew square to the bed, she gently pushed him backward. Andrew created a bounce as he assumed a sitting position on the bed, causing Miriam to partially awake.

In a dazed manner, Miriam said, "Baby, you're back."

Joan, still standing, straddled Andrew as he sat. She then sat on Andrew's legs and, with her hand, guided his to the warmth under Miriam's gown. Andrew's hand now operated on its own guidance system, taking a position between Miriam's thighs and continuing up to her jewel.

Miriam, now more awake, realized that it wasn't Joan's hand touching her.

Joan said, "Look, baby, I brought you something," as she massaged Miriam's breast. Andrew hearing Joan call Miriam "baby" in such an affectionate way and referring to him as an object caused him to lose his concentration, which also caused him to lose his erection. Andrew realized from their actions how much the two women were into each other. They were touching him, but they were touching each other, too. Joan started to undress Andrew and asked Miriam to help. That did the trick. Andrew snapped back to attention. Whatever was his initial apprehension was gone.

That was the first time that either of them had participated in a threesome. Their inexperience didn't cause a poor outcome though. In fact, the outcome was excellent. The two women had managed Andrew's assets perfectly, allowing everybody to be satisfied.

A few days later, Andrew's father regained consciousness and managed his goodbyes at his wife's funeral. It was a sad occasion, but the family got through it as families do. Luke took it the hardest. He had lost the wife whom he thought would be around to bury him. Luke would now require considerable time to recuperate, so Andrew persuaded Joan and Miriam to stay in Chicago so that he could be close to his father during this time. Andrew moved what had become his family into the main part of his father's house.

Andrew would go to the hospital every day. This day, when he entered his father's room, Luke was asleep. Andrew thought it was odd that he found himself in a situation that he caught a glimpse of as a kid but didn't understand at the time. Kathy was a flight attendant that lived with them when she was in town. Her family status changed in Andrew's mind, as he grew older. His parents and Kathy had a loving relationship for sure, but as time went on, Andrew understood better his parent's lifestyle. What he thought was a loving relationship among friends, was really a "love relationship between three people."

Things only became totally clear to Andrew when Kathy got pregnant with Luke's baby. That's when Kathy moved in full time and Luke and Ann cared for her until her baby was born.

With a sigh, Andrew thought about having two women to take care of in all the ways that a man was supposed to take care of a woman at a time that she was at her neediest.

Andrew's thoughts returned to the moment when he heard his father clear his throat. Luke awoke expressing typical morning moans and groans. He stretched and focused on the surroundings. His eyes took on a glow as they focused on Andrew standing near the door.

Lifestyle Change

Luke greeted his son in a voice still weak from his condition. "How are you, son?"

As Andrew moved toward his father, he said, "I'm fine, Dad." Once at his father's bedside, he gave him a hug.

Andrew and his father were close despite the fact that Luke conceived Andrew late in life. Luke had already raised four children to adulthood before Andrew and his twin sister were born. Now that Luke was laid up, he and Andrew talked even more than usual. During this recuperation period, Luke would do most of the talking. Andrew listened to his father and was amazed at his life. Of course, Andrew knew his father had children with five women, but he didn't know how much his father loved those women or that any one of them would have been the only woman in his father's life, if not for circumstances beyond his control.

As Luke talked about the women he loved, Andrew could see tears well in his father's eyes. When Luke talked about the children whom he and those women produced, Andrew could see the glow in those eyes.

That morning, as Luke appeared to be tiring of talk, his last words to Andrew were, "Regardless of your current status with your woman, you always do what's best for your children." A minute later, an attendant came in with Luke's breakfast tray, and less than a second after that Victoria entered the room. She spoke and continued on to the bathroom to wash her hands. When she came out of the bathroom, she stopped at Andrew and gave him a kiss on the cheek and continued on to Luke's bedside and gave him a kiss on the lips.

Victoria lifted the top from the breakfast tray and commented, "Let us see what we have for breakfast this morning."

After proper goodbyes, Andrew left. As he looked back and caught a glimpse of Victoria feeding his father, he understood better his father's last words. Andrew was on his way home now to do what was best for his children, even though they were still in their mother's bellies. That meant that he had to do what was best for Joan and Miriam too.

When Andrew returned home from the hospital, Joan and Miriam were still asleep in the big bed. He had left them two hours ago, promising to serve them breakfast when he returned. Andrew thought to himself that taking care of two women was a lot easier when they lived under the same roof and when they liked each other. Another factor making Andrew's job easier these days was the housekeeper/cook who had been with the family for years.

As Andrew stood looking at Joan and Miriam, who were in their sixth and seventh months, respectively, he realized at that moment they were more beautiful to him than ever. He watched them sleep until he couldn't resist touching them. When Andrew touched their bellies that had grown big, Miriam awoke immediately and her movements caused Joan to awake. The two beauties greeted each other before they greeted Andrew, but in unison, they invited him back to bed. Andrew, wanting to oblige, said, "I can't. One of you has a doctor's appointment in an hour. Who knows who has an appointment?"

Joan said, "It's me, and I'd forgotten."

Lifestyle Change

As he headed for the bathroom to start the shower, Andrew said, "That's okay. That's what I'm here for." As Andrew exited the bathroom, he declared, "Breakfast will be ready in ten minutes." He then gave the two beauties a kiss before leaving to check on progress in the kitchen.

Joan and Miriam were showered and dressed when Andrew returned and announced that breakfast was ready and that they needed to leave in ten minutes. Both women acknowledged that they were ready.

After leaving the doctor's office, they went shopping. Andrew enjoyed shopping with Joan and Miriam. They were his ladies. He sat back and offered suggestions as they tried on clothes. He liked seeing them looking good in the latest fashions. After shopping, they had lunch. Life was good for Andrew. He was living every man's dream. He had two beautiful women, who were no longer at his throat because of the other woman. They all made love together in such a balanced way that Andrew never grew tired. He thought to himself *things couldn't get much better than this.* Then he realized how much he was looking forward to becoming the father of three healthy babies at once. The fact that he had enough money to take care of them was icing on the cake. Their living as a threesome continued and even got better.

Months later Andrew and his ladies were playing spades. The usual stakes were that the winner would choose the night's activity. The stakes had been suspended since Miriam was expected to deliver any day now. She was given the choice of activity until she gave birth. Lately, Miriam preferred just cuddling. Sometimes, she and Joan would stay intertwined most of the night as if protecting each other from some danger. Even though Andrew sometimes felt excluded, he accepted the fact that their common condition automatically drew them closer together.

After their game, Andrew stayed behind while Joan and Miriam went ahead to get ready for bed. That's when things started to happen. Miriam was suddenly made aware that her baby was ready to be born.

Miriam said to Joan, "You'd better get Andrew, baby, it's time."

Joan was excited and moving in the wrong direction. She said to Miriam, "Stay calm. Everything is going to be okay."

Miriam, unlike Joan, was calm. She said to Miriam while pointing her to the door, "That way, babe, Andrew is that way."

"Oh yeah he's that way." Joan did manage to get Andrew, who had everything packed for days. Now all they had to do was get to the hospital. Miriam's contractions were at an interval that indicated they had time. When Joan and Miriam finished dressing, Andrew helped them into the backseat of the car.

The fact that A.J. was with his grandparents made things easier, prompting Andrew to comment to Joan, "I'm sure glad that A.J. is with your parents."

Joan responded in an urgent kind of way. "It really is good. I don't think I would be able to handle him and the two babies who just announced that they, too, are ready to be born."

Andrew kept his composure and kept his eyes on the road. It was most crucial that nothing delayed their getting to the hospital. Andrew asked, in a manner indicating that he would handle things no matter what the answer was, "Do we have time to make it or do I need to stop?" Andrew was glad when both his ladies indicated that he continues driving.

Miriam said, "These babies are going to be born in the hospital."

Andrew couldn't believe that both his ladies were ready to deliver at the same time, but real testament to the fact came only seconds later when Joan and Miriam, only seconds apart, wet their seats in preparation for the new arrivals.

When they arrived at the hospital, Andrew told Joan and Miriam to wait while he went for help. Within seconds, he returned with attendants with wheelchairs for Joan and Miriam. After being examined, it was determined that Miriam's delivery was progressing normally and that she would probably deliver sometime tonight. Joan was also progressing and expected to deliver soon, even though, she would be delivering prematurely. Joan and Miriam had different doctors, but both doctors worked out of this hospital. The attending nurse said that both doctors had been notified, and the only thing to do now was to wait until the babies were ready.

There was another expectant mother waiting for her baby to come. There was nobody with her at the time, and the nurse was busy doing something. Andrew noticed that the expecting mother was struggling to cover her feet but couldn't manage the task. Andrew asked if he could help. The woman accepted his offer. As he was adjusting the covers, the nurse jokingly said, "You're in for a busy night, Mr. Grant."

Luther C. Grayer

The nurse was correct about Andrew having a busy night ahead of him, but he only had to deal with Joan and Miriam. The other woman's husband came in minutes after Andrew had given his assistance.

Andrew was good at his coaching, having been through the Lamaze class three times now. He was looking forward to helping to bring these babies into the world.

It was three hours after they arrived at the hospital before the main action started. Joan and Miriam would probably disagree and say that the main action had started with their first labor pain.

Joan and Miriam remained in the same area while in labor. Andrew could be as helpful as possible with his two ladies together. He applied his Lamaze teachings well, and his occasional rub of requested areas was mentally soothing if nothing else.

When it came time to separate Joan and Miriam, Andrew asked himself. "What do I do now?"

The nurse said, "Stay with Ms. Chandler while we get Ms. Grant ready. She's almost ready to deliver."

Andrew panicked. He asked, "Who's about to deliver?"

"Your wife," the nurse replied. Then she said to Andrew, while looking at Joan, "I'll be back to get you before she delivers."

Andrew went to Joan's bedside and asked her, "What should do?"

Joan said, "Stay with Miriam now. I'll wait for you in the delivery room." As they were wheeling Joan away, she said to Miriam, "See you shortly, babe."

The nurse returned fifteen minutes later. "I'm going to take you to your wife now."

Andrew looked at Miriam. But before he could say anything, she said, "Go to her; I'll wait for you."

Joan delivered a boy forty minutes after being taken to the delivery room, and Andrew did something that he didn't do when his first son was born. He witnessed the birth of this son.

Two hours later, Andrew saw Miriam deliver him a third son. He had witnessed the birth of two sons in two hours by two women, but he had to wait another six hours before seeing Joan complete the delivery of twins. It was as if his daughter intended that her entrance into the world be adequately spaced from that of her two brothers. Joan was tired after delivering two babies over a span of eight hours. Her last words were, "I want to sleep."

Chapter Six

The Early Years
Two Women No Longer Pregnant

Hospitalized two days longer than Miriam, Joan was released from the hospital three days after giving birth. Luke was also released from the hospital around that time. He took up residence in Victoria's wing of his house and insisted that Victoria stay there with him. Luke had learned that Victoria needed to undergo radiation treatments to fight the return of the breast cancer that she had battled years ago. Even though Luke wasn't fully recovered from his accident, or from the death of his wife, he recognized that he was needed by someone he loved. As he had done all of his life, he stepped forward to be there for Victoria. He was determined to help her through her latest problem.

Now that Andrew had brought all of his family home, there were three generations of Grants occupying the big house. And, even though no plans had been made yet as to where Andrew and his contingents were going to live permanently, they would continue to stay there while they decided. Two nannies were hired to help take care of the three new babies and A.J. Andrew wanted his ladies to be able to get their rest or do whatever else they wanted to do. Lovemaking didn't resume for a while, but the first time that they did make love unfettered was very satisfying, both because it had been a while since they had done it and because Joan and Miriam were free for the first time to be as active as they wanted to be.

In the beginning, a big portion of Joan and Miriam's day dealt with feeding three new babies. Joan, of course, had the toughest job since she had two mouths to feed. And both were ready to eat at the same time. Sometimes, she actually had one on each breast at the same time, unwilling to make one wait while the other one ate.

Joan had wanted to have another baby so badly, but she was extremely depressed shortly after coming home from the hospital. Her relationship with Miriam had grown stronger since they had their babies. Sometimes Miriam was the only one who could get Joan through the day.

One day, while Joan and Miriam sat nursing all three babies, Joan started to cry. She sobbed that she was a bad mother for feeling the way she did. "I can't take it."

Miriam's son, Austin, had finished feeding and was sleeping in her lap. Miriam gave him to the nanny to put to bed, and then she went to Joan's side. She took Crystal, who had also finished feeding and was asleep. She gave her to the nanny to put to bed. Miriam hugged Joan while Christian continued to feed. Miriam told Joan that she was a good mother but that three babies were a lot to mentally deal with at any time but especially after just giving birth to twins. Miriam said emphatically, "You listen to me. I'm the psychology major here, and I know what I'm talking about. We're going to get you some help."

"I don't want to see anymore doctors," Joan sobbed. She was almost hysterical in her insistence. "Please don't make me go. I want to talk to you. Can I talk to you?" The exuberance with which Joan protested disturbed Christian, who had fallen asleep like his brother and sister had earlier.

As Miriam took Christian from Joan's arms, she softly said, "You can always talk to me, babe, you know that. I love you." She gave Christian to the nanny so he could be put to bed.

"You never said that you loved me before."

"I know, but I've felt it for a long time, and I know you knew that. Now come and lie down, I want you to rest for a while." Miriam led Joan to the bed and tucked her in. "You get some sleep now."

"Yeah, before my babies are ready to eat again." Joan was asleep within a minute of her head touching the pillow. Miriam went to the living room and was just in time to greet Andrew as he was returning with A.J. from a doctor's appointment. A.J., unlike his siblings, was wide-awake and ready for play. The nanny, having heard them come-in, was there immediately to take A.J., leaving Andrew and Miriam alone.

"We've got to get her some help."

Andrew knew exactly what Miriam was saying. He had already spoken to Joan's doctor who recommended a psychologist, but only if the idea of Joan seeing another doctor didn't upset her more. Some people suffered more because of being forced to see a doctor than from their actual condition. It's called McGrusom's Syndrome. It was thought to be an extreme form of postpartum depression.

Andrew told Miriam, "When I mentioned her seeing another doctor, she said that she didn't want to see no doctor. She was almost panic-stricken when I said she had to, so I didn't push it."

"That's the same reaction I just got. I wonder what she has against doctors."

"I don't know," Andrew said as A.J. re-entered the room with his nanny. A.J. ran straight for his dad. Andrew lifted his son as high as he could and said, "Maybe she needs a vacation away from these babies. Maybe both of you do."

One day, after the babies had finished nursing, it could be heard in her voice that Joan's condition had worsened. She said, with great sadness, "I don't have anything left."

Miriam, with a puzzled look, asked, "What do you mean, baby?"

Pausing to sniffle between every other word, Joan mumbled, "I don't think I have any more milk. I'm not sure Christian got enough."

Miriam was quick to respond. "We know he got enough because he went to sleep. That's what babies do, they get full and they go to sleep." After a pause Miriam said, "You still have plenty of milk left. I can see that by the bulge of your breast. Everything happens bigger when you have two babies at once including anxiety." Miriam then sat beside Joan and began to extract milk from her breast using the breast pump that the nanny had left. "Does that hurt?"

"No, it feels good, I should see that doctor that you and Andrew want me to see so he can tell me why I'm acting so crazy."

Joan did see a doctor, but she continued to be depressed. Andrew decided that his idea of a vacation away from the children was worth trying. He convinced Joan and Miriam that they could benefit from some time away from the children. Joan worried about what her babies and Austin would eat during their absence. She believed in the benefits of breast-feeding. Andrew had already checked and found that there were companies that delivered small quantities of perishable products, such as baby formula, across the country within a few hours of pick-up. Joan and Miriam accepted the vacation plan and decided to travel back to Boston where so much had happened for them.

The day before they were to leave for Boston, Joan and Miriam sat talking. Joan was lamenting that she was making it necessary that they leave their children. "I'm sorry that I'm causing you to leave your son, Austin."

Miriam said, "You really don't understand do you? I would have been gone by now if not for you."

"You were going to take Austin and go?"

"No I was just going to leave and let Andrew raise Austin. I was going to do as the female penguin does after she lays her fertilized egg. She leaves everything else to the male penguin to take care of including raising the offspring." Their conversation was interrupted when Andrew entered the room carrying Christian and Austin, who were ready for lunch. Andrew said, "Crystal is still sleeping. I'll feed her later from the supply of stored milk."

Joan said, "No! Bring her to me when she's ready to eat. I'll be ready." She thought in silence *I've got to get well so that I can get back to my babies.*

Andrew, feeling Joan's pain, assured her that he would take care of everything while they were gone. "Just concentrate on you for now, and let me worry about everything else." Joan's only reply was a sad "Okay."

The first few days in Boston were great, and both women were beginning to believe that this vacation time was what Joan needed, but that feeling didn't last. Even though they made love at leisure and enjoyed each other's company immensely, something was missing.

One day, while they walked the campus of the college, they stopped to observe an almost all male class being conducted outdoors. Both women were instantly stimulated, as if something deep within their core was energized. Joan was so affected by the professor's lecture that she was compelled to respond to the question that he posed to determine if he had succeeded in making his points understood. The professor, seeing only the hand of a female stranger relentless in its attempt to get his attention, made a joke that caused the class to laugh.

The professor said to his mostly male student body, "You see, it only takes a few minutes to understand Justin's complex Theory of Root Orientation, and this young lady is here to prove it."

As Joan proceeded to answer the professor's question, showing that she did understand the complex theory, the laughter ceased. The professor was so impressed that he invited Joan to sit in on future sessions.

Joan accepted the professor's offer and monitored the class for the remainder of the semester. Dentistry 101 was the beginning of her love for the dental profession. Miriam found herself a class in psychology to monitor. It was during that class that she learned more about The McGrusom Syndrome, a complex theory to be debated for some time to come. The theory might offer a cure for Joan's severe anxiety, but the recommended cure was guaranteed to cause alarm from men everywhere.

Joan and Miriam planned to return home at the end of the semester which was only another two weeks. But, at the end of the semester, they signed up to take classes for credit during the summer semester. They didn't return home that semester preferring instead to pursue the more stimulating life of academia. Things were going well for them.

Andrew accepted the fact that they wanted to keep things the way they were for a while longer and not have him and the kids join them yet. He had to make due with Joan and Miriam's occasional trips home for his sexual release. He did occasionally manage to go to Boston, but that was only when his sister was home from school and could stay with his children. Andrew wasn't ready to leave the children alone with the hired help. Even though Luke was in the house, he had his hands full with Victoria as she was recovering from surgery due to her breast cancer.

There was a two-week break between the end of the summer semester and the beginning of the fall semester, and Andrew was expecting that his women spend that time at what was still their home in Chicago. He was surprised when Miriam asked him to have their milk picked-up in California for the next week while they participated in a seminar for women aspiring to be future leaders.

Finally, Joan and Miriam did return home for a two-week period. They didn't attempt to breast feed their children since it had been difficult to wane them in the short period of time they had before leaving for Boston. All three babies had adjusted well to getting the nourishment of their mother's milk from a bottle, but as Joan and Miriam participated in feeding them, something happened. They realized how much they missed their babies.

Joan said, "I don't want to be away from my babies anymore."

"Okay," Miriam replied, "Let's take them with us."

"Andrew will be glad that finally we'll all be together again. He has been anxious for a while now."

"I was thinking that just you, I, and the children go," Miriam said. "We can give Andrew a break from things for a while."

Miriam's proposal took Joan by surprise, but she realized that it was merely an extension of what they had already started doing; Andrew was being eliminated from their lives.

Joan asked, "Why are we pushing Andrew out? Why can't we keep things the way they were just before the babies were born? Things were good then, weren't they?"

Miriam didn't answer Joan's question; she remembered how depressed Joan had been and how much better she was now. She just needed her babies for a while and no man. That would give her time to get completely well.

Andrew offered support to his father, who had now lost three loves in less than six months and was vulnerable. Yes, Victoria died shortly after her surgery and Luke seemed finally whipped and ready to give up. When Miriam suggested that Andrew stay to look after his father while she and Joan take the kids back to Boston with them, Andrew agreed; he figured he would be joining them soon.

Andrew hired a private duty nurse to help care for his father, and Joan and Miriam returned to Boston, but this time they had their babies with them.

In Boston, things went well. Joan and Miriam had adequate help with the kids; they had brought the children's nannies with them which allowed them to continue their success in their studies.

One day, during her sociology class, Miriam's answer to her professor's question demonstrated how much her thinking had changed. It was as different as her new hair color, which was bright red. Since giving birth, it seemed that she had reevaluated the role of the male in the life of the female in today's society. Her philosophy that the eligible men had to be shared remained the center of her contentions. His sperm was needed, but she had now progressed to the belief that once he had provided the sperm, he was no longer needed on a full-time basis. He would be able to continue his role as a roaming procreator. The affected females could then band together and raise the offspring produced by the roamer. Men enjoy variety so much that they cheat anyway.

There was laughter by mostly male members of the class when they realized that Miriam's view of society allowed them to love as many women as they wanted seemingly without commitment or consequence. Only after her statement that the male's ability to play would be determined by his ability to pay did the female members of the class have their turn at laughter. The ring of the bell ended the class discussion, postponing further view of Miriam's society, which seemed to be continuously developing.

That night, Joan lay awake in bed after Miriam had fallen asleep. They made love earlier and Miriam's effort to please Joan was so apparent that Joan didn't have to do anything. She was allowed to enjoy Miriam's efforts to both women's complete satisfaction. This was not new, but especially lately. It was as if Miriam was trying to prove that a man wasn't necessary for their sexual fulfillment.

Andrew helped his father get over his grief. The excellent medical care from his private duty nurse, Gina, played a large part in the recovery. Luke had come to recognize again that life was for the living and that he still had things to do. He thanked his son for his help during tough times, but now he encouraged Andrew to rejoin his family. It had been more than two months that Andrew had been separated from his children and he was anxious to get back to them. Before Andrew could join his family, he received the letter that rocked his world. The letter was a request for a divorce.

Andrew traveled to Boston a number of times to try to convince Joan not to divorce him. He finally had to accept what seemed to be his fate. It was over between him and Joan. When the divorce proceedings began, it was a time of Andrew's deepest despair. He was helped through that time by his first romantic experience with an older woman. She had been around for sometime now. Gina was the beautiful private duty nurse that Andrew had hired to help with his father. She was old enough to be Andrew's mother. Perhaps Gina's motherly instincts caused her to want to ease Andrew's pain. Mothers are good at that, but more than likely it was Gina's womanly instincts operating too. Andrew was quite a hunk.

Gina was married, but she and her husband, Leroy McGee, were continually breaking up and making up. Even though Gina was no longer needed as a nurse, she and Andrew continued to spend time together. Andrew saw Gina in a different light now that he had been betrayed by two young women. Gina was his refuge.

The mutual attraction between them grew now that they were both available. Gina's husband was in jail, as he was often. He was a petty criminal that seemed destined to do big time.

The first time that Gina and Andrew made love was the night that Gina found Andrew crying like a baby. He thought he was alone. Actually, he was alone until Gina entered his part of the house without him knowing it. She knocked on his door but got no answer. She figured he was asleep but she needed to tell him that she was about to leave for the night. When Andrew realized he was not alone, he made some untrue excuse for his tears, but Gina knew why he was really crying. She'd been where Andrew was now. She had lost lovers too and what she wanted at the time was her lover back, but since that wasn't possible, she wanted someone to hug her who understood what she was going through. Gina took a seat next to Andrew on the sofa and gave him the big hug that she would want if she were yearning for her lost love.

Two Women No Longer Pregnant

What happened next was predictable. With Andrew's head resting on Gina's shoulder, his lips were so close to hers that they couldn't resist making contact. It was like opposite poles of two magnets when their lips made contact, locking tightly. Their hands explored each other's body and when Gina's breasts were exposed, they became an even more powerful magnet. They caused Andrew's lips to abandon Gina's lips and lock onto them. Andrew nursed one breast and then the other, as if trying to decide which one was more delicious. Andrew wondered if Gina's age had anything to do with the softness of her body. He had never felt a body that soft before. Every part he touched, and he touched them all, were softer than the finest down and when he finally climbed aboard, he thought to himself, *this must be what it would be like if you could float on a cloud.*

Andrew had been sexually active for quite a while but he learned things from Gina that he didn't know. That old adage — you can't teach an old dog new tricks — was probably true, but Andrew was not an old dog. Even though he had been sexually active for quite a while, he was a young man and there were things for him to learn, and Gina was an excellent teacher. Andrew didn't confine his new sexual prowess to just Gina. He spread it around.

One day, while Andrew was demonstrating some of his new knowledge to a lovely young thing, Gina paid him an unannounced visit. That was the day he hurt her. Normally, Andrew wouldn't answer the door when entertaining. He was smarter than that. But this day he was expecting a package and thought it was the deliveryman. He opened the door in his robe and was surprised to see Gina standing there. She had an arm full of take out food.

Beaming, Gina said, "Surprise; I brought you something to eat, baby."

Andrew was truly surprised. "Gina, why didn't you call?"

It didn't take Gina long to realize that Andrew had company. She put the food down and turned to leave. As she departed, she said, "I'm sorry. I should have called."

Andrew wanted to stop Gina, but what could he say? *Ah, ah listen, baby. I've got this other woman in my bed.* No, there was nothing he could say. He had hurt her and he didn't like the way it made him feel.

It took Andrew a couple of days to do what he needed to do. When he called Gina, she was still alive; she was still eating and doing all the other things that she needed to do. Andrew realized that, yes, life was complicated and sometimes we got hurt, but we can take it. To hurt sometimes was to know you're alive. He apologized to Gina, a person that he loved but was not in love with. He also thanked her for helping him through a tough period and he told her that he would be there if she ever needed him.

Gina accepted things for what they were. They had some good sex, but now it was over and they were friends who could call on each other if they needed to. Gina and Andrew didn't engage in sex after that and a month later, Joan and Andrew were granted a divorce.

Looking back at the situation, one has to ask how such a thing could have happened. For sure, Andrew pondered that question. The only answer might be that the combination of events set up the scenario that led to an outcome as unexpected as this. In what seemed like an instant, Andrew had lost his wife to his woman. That's a hell of a thing.

Andrew lost his wife and his woman but he didn't lose his children. The court awarded him joint custody of all four of them. Andrew agreed to continue to support Joan and Miriam in the manner that they had become accustomed, even though the court could only require Andrew to contribute a portion of his earnings, and Andrew's earnings now were zero.

Andrew would be a rich man one day, but now, he was just the son of a rich man and without his voluntary contribution, he couldn't be made to support the two women that bore him children. The words of Andrew's father stayed with him through out this entire ordeal. "Regardless of your current status with your woman, you always do what's best for your children." Andrew was operating on that premise when he agreed to support the mothers of his children. He would even eventually find a place in the Boston area to make the transfer easier for the children from one parent to the other.

After moving to Boston, Andrew continued wooing lots of women, but he was determined not to get hung up on any one of them. Life as a single man was good. Andrew reaped the full benefit. He had money, he was handsome, and he had a place to take the numerous women that were at his beck and call. He now questioned why he ever wanted to be tied to one woman anyway.

Audrey was one of the many women that Andrew was seeing. When Andrew realized that he was beginning to feel more for

Audrey than he ever intended to feel for a woman again, he cut her loose. He was particularly cruel when he broke up with Audrey. In a nonchalant manner, he told her that he had other women that he was more interested in seeing. Andrew's statement was meant to hurt so that Audrey would just go away. Audrey was hurt. She sat crying after having finally caught up with Andrew to get this harsh explanation as to why he had stopped seeing her.

Who knows why a woman's tears affect a man in such a powerful way. Unlike Andrew's words that were meant to hurt, Audrey's tears weren't. They were her response to the hurt that she felt and was not an attempt to retaliate, but retaliate they did. They caused Andrew the kind of pain that he had felt when he realized he had lost Joan.

Andrew didn't stand a chance of succeeding at getting Audrey out of his mind. Just because you break up with someone doesn't mean it's over. Even though it had only been two months since they met, this beautiful woman had his nose open from the beginning. It's been song about a lot; a heart does what it wants to, and there is nothing you can do about it.

Andrew was only able to hold out for a week before begging his way back into Audrey's life.

Why does a woman's tears affect a man so strongly, but especially if he loves her? When a man does something that was hurtful to his woman, there was a need within him to hold her in his arm and make things right. A woman's tears are powerful, conquering the strongest of men. Andrew hadn't thought he would ever love another woman as he loved Joan, but Audrey had changed that. Things had ended between Andrew and Joan and had begun for him and Audrey. Andrew and Audrey got married during a double ceremony with Angela and Walter, Joan's brother. The ceremony was hosted by Luke. Joan's presence at her brother's and her ex-husband's double wedding was testament that forever wasn't always in the cards. She had divorced Andrew and he had moved on. Andrew now had a new mate. Ten months after Andrew and Audrey were married came a six-pound baby girl.

Andrew sat looking at Audrey while she slept. She had worked hard giving birth to their daughter. The birth for Andrew was no less spectacular than the ones he had witnessed three years earlier when he saw three of his children born in a matter of hours. Each one represented something special just as the birth of his first child had. Now this fifth one takes on that same special quality. Andrew felt an awesome responsibility but was confident in his ability to live up to those responsibilities. His latest child was named Ann after Andrew's deceased mother.

Andrew had already received the news of another birth that had occurred a year earlier. Gina, the beautiful private duty nurse, had given birth to a son. Eugene was Andrew's fourth son.

Chapter Seven

The Early Years
Crime and Punishment

It was a chilly Boston day when the police arrested Miriam. She and Joan were having lunch on campus when two detectives approached them. They said that they were investigating the homicide of an assistant professor killed ten months ago. It was the gold charm, scribed in the form of the letters L.O.V.E., found next to the body that caused police to want to talk to Miriam. They had traced the charm back to a jeweler, who no longer lived in the country and was only recently located. The jeweler's records showed that Miriam had purchased the charm more than a year before the killing.

It didn't take much investigation after tracing the charm to learn of the past relationship between Miriam and the victim. Miriam became an even greater suspect when detectives talked to the landlord of the building where she once lived. He told them of the stormy relationship between Miriam and the victim before she moved. He even recalled seeing them tussling outside one morning until another male approached causing Mr. Minor to run away. It was also learned that the victim, Mr. Minor, had

Crime and Punishment

spread malicious rumors concerning the identity of the father of Miriam's baby. Because of those rumors, she had to quit her job.

Mr. Minor had been shot once in the chest, the bullet piercing his heart, killing him instantly. Police decided to arrest Miriam when a witness was found who saw a redheaded woman about her height entering the victim's building the day of the killing.

After the police took Miriam away, Joan took a cab to Andrew's apartment. Miriam was a frequent driver of Joan's car, so the police confiscated it to check for evidence.

When Joan arrived at Andrew's apartment, the head nanny was the only one working. When she answered the doorbell, she was surprised to see Joan. In a panic, she asked, "Are the kids supposed to be ready?"

"No, the kids are fine," and then she asked anxiously, "Is Andrew home?" He was there, and luckily, this was one of those rare instances when all the children were asleep except for baby Ann, who was being nursed by her mother. Andrew was free to listen, as Joan told him what had happened. At the end of her periodic hysterical utterances, she pleaded with Andrew for help. "You have to help her Andrew. She didn't do this."

"How do you know she didn't do it? Morris was her ex-lover or maybe he was still her lover," Andrew said. "She may have killed him for some reason you don't even know." He continued, as if this was the perfect opportunity to get some things off his chest. "Lovers fall out of love all the time and sometimes they even kill with a swiftness and permanency that might be considered humane, not like those who would kill by withholding their love and eventually leave causing a slow and painful death."

Joan could tell that the pain she and Miriam had caused Andrew was still there. "I'm sorry for the hurt we caused you Andrew, but Miriam saved me. I was dying and she saved me."

Andrew coldly said, "That's good. I'm glad that she saved you from a monster like me, but there's nothing I can do to save her." As if on cue, Austin was the first of Andrew's sleeping brood to arise demanding some attention.

Austin's sound was unmistakable prompting Joan to ask, "What about your son Austin? What will he think of you when he's old enough to realize that you refused to help his mother?"

Andrew asked sarcastically, "What am I supposed to do if she killed the man? Hell, she probably just snapped."

"She didn't Andrew. I know that. But, whatever is the truth, she needs the best legal help possible, and you have the money to make that happen. Your father knows the people to hire."

The mentioning of his father caused Andrew to remember the quote that his father had lived by all his life. The quote resounded in Andrew's head, *Regardless of your current status with your woman, you always do what's best for your children.*

Austin's babblings got stronger as if he was insisting that Andrew help his mother. All the children were now awake and clamoring, seemingly in support of Joan and Austin's attempt to get help for Miriam. Joan asked if she could see the children before leaving. It was as if she needed to thank them for their support. That's when they were joined by Audrey, still holding baby Ann, who had now finished nursing and seemed ready to join her brothers and sister in whatever was the day's activities.

This was the first time that Joan and Audrey had seen each

other since the wedding, ten months ago, and it was the first time that Joan had seen Audrey's new baby.

Joan said, "She's beautiful."

"I agree, she is beautiful," Audrey responded, "she looks like her sister, Crystal, to me." Joan acknowledged Audrey's compliment that her daughter, Crystal, was beautiful too. Audrey then said, "I thought the children would be here for the whole month."

"They will. I'm not here to pick them up. I came to tell Andrew that Austin's mother has been arrested."

Audrey responded with shock "Miriam has been arrested; what ever for?"

After Joan explained things to Audrey, Audrey joined Joan in pleading to Andrew for help for Miriam. Talk of Miriam's plight had to stop though, as all five of the children were now demanding more attention than the one nanny could give. Joan, Andrew and Audrey all joined in to care for the children.

In the end, Andrew agreed to provide the help for Miriam, but it wasn't because of Joan. Audrey's forcefulness eventually persuaded him to act.

Andrew sought the advice of his father, who hired attorney Max Savior to coordinate Miriam's defense. Max had worked for Andrew's father for many years on an array of legal matters. He was good at what he did. He was real good. Even though Attorney Savior's law practice was in Chicago, he had contacts all over the country. Mr. Savior established a co-defense by joining forces with an excellent criminal attorney named Singer that he knew in the Boston area. They both had worked with an investigator who was also excellent at what he did. His name was Bob Goodman.

Luther C. Grayer

Once the trial started, it took a month. Sometimes, no matter how good a person's legal team is, or how deep their pockets, if the evidence against them is strong enough, a good prosecutor would win. The evidence against Miriam, though circumstantial, was very strong. In fact, it grew stronger when eyewitness picked Miriam out of a lineup, as the woman entering Morris' building, two days before his death. A tenant of the building testified to hearing Morris arguing with a female shortly after Miriam was seen entering the building. That, coupled with the fact that another witness, though not able to identify Miriam personally, did report seeing a woman her size and with her hair color entering Morris' building the same day that he was killed.

Miriam had said that she hadn't seen Morris since they broke up four years ago. The eyewitness testimony placing her in Morris' building two days before his murder was a big blow to the defense. In the end, the jury convicted Miriam of second-degree murder based on the abundance of circumstantial evidence.

It took three months from the time Miriam was first arrested to the time she was tried and convicted. She had been out on bail, but now, she was locked in a tiny jail cell. During Miriam's first few nights in jail, the guard would tap on her cell bars requesting that she put on a show for him. He had promised her privileges in return for her becoming his showgirl. That's what they did to the new prisoners. Miriam told him where to put his privileges.

At night, the guard continued to tap on the bars and Miriam continued to offer the ultimate defiance. She pretended to be asleep. The guard left time after time unable to get his jollies. Miriam wished that she had done the same thing to Morris instead of allowing herself to be blackmailed by such a repugnant man.

Crime and Punishment

While in jail, Miriam had time to reminisce. One day as she sat in the tiny cell, her thoughts carried her back in time and she replayed in her mind how this mess got started:

It was four years ago that she first met Miss Dynamite. That was before Miriam conceived of her scheme to get pregnant with Andrew's baby. She hadn't even met Andrew then, nor had she met Joan.

Miss Dynamite was the nickname that Miriam gave the woman who became her lover. Miriam had just broken up with Morris and was now alone. Miss Dynamite was in the park that night with her boyfriend, who was upset with her about something; he was threatening to whip her ass. People passed the couple not willing to get involved even when it became obvious that this six-foot, two-hundred-pound male was on the verge of physical violence towards this petite woman. Miriam thought maybe she could prevent an escalation to violence if she made it clear to this big guy that the four-foot-eight-inch woman wouldn't be alone if he hit her. Miriam figured, if it came to a fight, she and the petite miss could give this jerk, posing as a man, a run for his money. Miriam said as cool as she could, "Calm down, Mister. Don't you hit her or you'll have to fight us both."

Though shocked, the boyfriend responded, "Stay out of this you bitch, or I'll kick your ass too."

That's when Miss Dynamite showed her explosiveness. Her personality changed dramatically. She went from seeming like a meek lovely lady to somebody you didn't want to mess with.

She got everybody's attention when she shouted, "You sorry ass excuse of a man. If you touch either one of us, you had better kill me. If you don't, I swear on my mother's grave I'll kill you." She continued with coldness. "You won't be able to close your eyes, because if you do you'll wake up one night and find me in your chest. And I'll be the last person you'll ever see."

Anybody hearing this petite dynamo would be inclined to believe that she would do just what she said, and nobody believed it more than her boyfriend. He made his exit while shouting profanities, willing to let that suffice for the physical violence he would have rendered to a less formidable opponent. This woman was nobody's prey.

Miriam and Miss Dynamite talked for a long time that evening and continued to get acquainted over the next couple of weeks. Miriam learned that Miss Dynamite had come from a home that was headed by another of the world's bullies. Her stepfather was a male perpetrating a man; he beat Miss Dynamite's mother, who was all of a hundred pounds. In Miss Dynamite's mind, though not in the mind of the court, her mother died because of the beatings she suffered. Miss Dynamite was thirteen when her mother died. At age fourteen, she vowed that no man would ever misuse her without paying the cost. She grew up on her own since her stepfather died after falling down the stairs of their home less than a year after her mother's death.

Miriam's sex life became a matter of intense interest to Miss Dynamite when she learned that Miriam had been with a woman before. Miss Dynamite said, "I guess all men are dogs, is that why you tried a woman?"

"I suppose I was having man problems at the time, but all men aren't dogs. Most of the good ones might be taken, but there are good men out there."

Then Miss Dynamite showed her naiveté when she asked, while blushing, "How does it work? How do two women do it?"

Miriam responded to the questions with a question not believing that Miss Dynamite was serious. "How does what work?"

"You know what I mean. We've got the same thing. They don't fit."

Miriam said, "A woman can do all the things to another woman that a man can except get her pregnant."

Miss Dynamite, while indicating total disbelief, said, "I don't believe that. You have to show me!"

Miriam was surprised again and attempted to make a joke. "Are you from Missouri?"

Miss Dynamite merely grinned at Miriam's comedic effort and made it obvious that she was still waiting for a real answer.

Even though Miriam had been surprised by Miss Dynamite's request, she was also aroused by it. "Do you want me to show you now, right here?"

"No. I want you to take me out and seduce me. You said a woman can do everything a man can except get her pregnant, and I'm not interested in getting pregnant."

Miriam and Miss Dynamite had dinner that night, and they made love for the first time. They continued as lovers for more than a month, but one day Miss Dynamite just left. Shortly after that, Miriam came up with her scheme to get pregnant with Andrew's baby.

What makes one cheat on their mate? Miriam had asked herself that question a number of times and didn't know the answer. She hadn't planned to cheat on Joan, but she was faced with temptation when Miss Dynamite reappeared. It was temptation that she couldn't pass up.

It had been more than four years since Miriam had seen her former lover, but there was an instant reconnection when the two women were reunited a year ago; this despite the fact that Miriam was then involved with Joan. That was the beginning of Miriam's affair with two women at the same time. It was at that time that Miriam gave Miss Dynamite a charm.

After Miriam and Miss Dynamite's relationship rekindled, another person from Miriam's past reappeared. Miriam hadn't seen her ex-boyfriend, Morris, for more than three years until his return a year ago. His opening comment to Miriam then was how are you and your two lovers doing?

Miriam now knows that if you cheat, there is always the possibility that somebody will see you. Well, that's what happened to her. Morris had seen her around the campus with both Joan and Miss Dynamite but never with both women at the same time. With minor surveillance, Morris put two and two together and got three. He threatened to tell all unless Miriam paid him.

Paying the money wasn't bad. It was the other that made Miriam's flesh crawl. The feel of Morris' touch and the smirk on his face that said I can make you do anything I want. When he

Crime and Punishment

proceeded to prove that he could make her do what he wanted, Miriam closed her eyes, which allowed her to pretend that it wasn't happening. She couldn't pretend anymore when she felt Morris inside her. She had had sex with him before, but this time it caused her to feel dirty.

Despite the seriousness of the times, Miriam had to laugh to herself when she recalled how some things never change. Morris Minor was as quick as ever, in and out in three minutes flat. "At least that was a blessing," she reminisced.

After that one time, Miriam told Morris that he wasn't going to screw her again and that's when they had their big fight. Morris didn't screw anybody again long after that. A couple of days later, he was dead.

Miriam's thoughts returned to the present when she heard her cell door opening. It was time for lunch.

After Miriam's conviction, Joan had a lot of free time too. She was home alone a lot. One day Joan was rearranging furniture in the room where the children played when they were home. She found jewelry under a chair that she had moved from the corner. One of the pieces of jewelry was Miriam's charm. It was the same as the charm that the police allegedly found next to Morris' body and was the piece of evidence that had led them to Miriam.

Joan was excited since her finding the charm at home should have some positive bearing on Miriam's case.

The next day when Joan showed Miriam the charm and told her where she had found it, Miriam was surprised. She thought that she had really lost it during her visit to Morris' place.

Luther C. Grayer

Joan, with excitement in her voice, said, "Your lawyer should be able to prove that this is your charm and not the one that the police found at the murder scene."

Miriam thought in silence, *she's right, if I didn't lose my charm at Morris' place, then it might be the one I gave to Miss Dynamite, and if Morris had tried to blackmail her, she would have killed him.*

Joan, not getting the excited response from Miriam that she had anticipated said, "This is good news. Isn't this good news?" Still not receiving a response from Miriam, Joan sighed. "Come on, Miriam give me something. Tell me what you're thinking."

Miriam didn't want to tell Joan what she was thinking. She knew it would hurt her to know that she had bought two charms and had given one to her other lover.

Miriam didn't tell Joan that she had bought two charms but she knew now that she had to tell her lawyer. She told Joan to take the charm to Attorney Singer and tell him that she needed to see him as soon as possible.

As Joan was about to leave, she said, "I almost forgot. When I stopped by Andrew's place this morning to see the kids, I told him and Audrey about the charm. Audrey was excited. She asked me to ask you if it would be okay for her to visit."

Miriam replied, "I'll be here."

Attorney Singer was at the jail early the next morning. He had news himself that had bearing on Miriam's case. His investigator had found the city inspector responsible for the yearly inspection of the building that Mr. Minor was found dead in. She was a stunning red head about Miriam's height. Her records indicated that she was at the building the day that Mr. Minor was killed.

Crime and Punishment

Miriam responded with excitement. "That proves that I was telling the truth about not being there that day."

"Not exactly, but the fact that another redhead was at the building the day of the killing means to a judge that there is reason for a new trial." He then said, "Joan told me where she found this charm. Statistic show that people that lose jewelry have usually misplaced it somewhere at home. Is that what you did?"

Miriam took a deep breath and said, "No, I didn't tell you the complete truth. I bought two charms and gave one to a friend."

Mr. Singer didn't interrupt Miriam. He listened as she explained. She had lied to him before about seeing Morris and now she was telling him of another lie.

At the end of their session, Attorney Singer didn't need to tell his client how dumb she had been. She now knew how it was to tell her lawyer anything but the complete truth from the start. As Mr. Singer was about to leave, Miriam asked, "What should I do if she comes to see me?"

Singer responded in a nonchalant way. "See her. She can't hurt you in here."

Later that same day, Miriam was paid a visit by Audrey. The two women hadn't seen each other since the last day of Miriam's trial. They now sat facing each other with the thick glass between them. At first, they communicated without words. Then Audrey said, "I heard that Joan found a charm at home."

"Yes she did, which means it wasn't my charm that they found beside Morris' body. Then with emphasis Miriam asked, "Is it the charm I gave you, Miss Dynamite?"

Audrey, with no hesitation said, "No, it's not the one you gave me. I'm sure of that. I just misplaced mine a month ago after taking it off so I could have the clasp on my bracelet fixed."

Miriam said, "I didn't kill Morris, and if I lost my charm at home, then the one that the police found must be the one I gave you."

"I didn't kill the man either. I didn't even know him," said Audrey.

Miriam countered by saying, "You didn't know Andrew either until I told you about him, and now look at you. You're married to him and have his baby."

"Don't hate me, Miriam, because I wanted the same things you had; a baby by a good man. And he wasn't even taken when I screwed him; unlike he was when you did." Audrey said again, "I had my charm a month ago. Joan's daughter loved playing with it, while I held her and Ann together."

"It's too bad that Crystal is too young to verify your story. I guess DNA tests will have to prove whose charm was found next to Morris' body. My lawyer knows that I gave you a charm"

Three days later, Miriam was released from jail on bond while she waited for a new trial. A new trial had been granted based primarily on final notice of a parking ticket that Joan got in the mail two days ago. Three notices had been sent earlier but to the wrong address. Miriam had testified in court that she had driven Joan's car to Alibi Park, which was twenty miles from where Mr. Minor was killed. She said that she had seen three boys playing around the car when she returned from her walk in the park. Investigators working on the case weren't able to locate any boys who would corroborate Miriam's story, but the ticket now proved that the car that Miriam often drove was at the park at the time of the killing.

Miriam was home again. Tonight, she was sleeping in her own bed for the first time in over a month. When her head assumed a comfortable position on her pillow her future came into focus.

Miriam was acquitted of Morris' death and Audrey was convicted of the crime. Miriam convinced Joan to forgive her for cheating. Joan was strong with no signs of the postpartum depression that would have destroyed her earlier. Joan accepted the fact that she had been cheated on again. It was no big thing.

Miriam had successfully pulled off the recommended cure for the McGrusom Syndrome, which was the radical extraction of the patient from her male mate who was the source of her anxiety. Miriam took credit for having gotten Joan away from the situation that had made her ill. It was the only way to cure her.

Miriam didn't want Joan to get a divorce from Andrew, but when Joan insisted on taking things to the next level, Miriam realized that she had no choice but to go along with whatever Joan wanted. Joan had to feel that she was completely free of Andrew before she could deal with the confusion that existed in her head or deal with a male as a mate again.

Miriam had cured Joan of her illness. But in the process, she had hurt Andrew badly and now he had also lost Audrey. Andrew's loneliness was so overwhelming that Miriam felt sorry for him, not to mention guilty. She had taken Joan from him and had made him a target for Audrey and now he was womanless. The fact that there was the welfare of the children to consider, Miriam was determined to help Andrew through this bad time. She knew he was angry with her. He may even have hated her, but that wasn't going to stop her from doing what she could to help her baby's daddy.

It had been four months since Audrey was convicted of killing Morris and Andrew continued to be sad. He and Miriam were talking regularly now.

One day while the children were with the nannies at Andrew's apartment, Miriam convinced Andrew to come to her place to put together a toy that she had bought for them. When Andrew got there, Miriam was nervously waiting. She opened the door and immediately began to execute her plan. She encircled Andrew with both arms holding him tight. It was a defensive maneuver to prevent him from doing what she was about to give him permission to do. She closed her eyes tight while she buried her head in his chest. She then said, "Okay, you can knock me on my ass if you want to. I know you think that I deserve it."

Miriam waited for Andrew to act. After realizing that he wasn't going to take her up on her offer, Miriam said in the sweetest tone, "Let me help you through this."

It had been a while since Andrew had been in the arms of a woman, and this woman knew the combination to unlock his manhood. After starting the process, Miriam tried to slow things down so that she could execute the other part of her plan. Maybe if she had thought to wear pants instead of a dress it would have taken Andrew longer to get to her jewel. Just as he was about to strip her of her panties, she heard the key enter the lock to the front door. Joan thought to herself, *thank goodness she's home!*

When Joan entered the apartment, Miriam said, "Hi, baby, look what's here," as she pointed at Andrew's protruding manhood. Joan looked at the bulge between Andrew's legs before running to the bedroom slamming the door behind her.

Andrew, now deflated in more ways than one, spoke with anger, "What the hell are you trying to do with this amateur psychology stuff? You'll have us all in a mental institution."

Miriam braced herself wondering if Andrew had reconsidered her offer inviting him to knock her on her behind. Miriam was relieved once again when Andrew didn't take her up on her offer. She said, "I wanted to show her and you that she can do this again and that you're the man that she should do it with."

As Andrew was about to leave, the door to the bedroom swung open and they could see Joan. She walked to the king sized bed and lay across it face down still fully clothed. Andrew stood looking not knowing what to do; Miriam took his hand and led him to the big bed. She guided Andrew to the prize that lay in wait. Joan's jewel was easy to get to since she too was wearing a dress.

Miriam, feeling that she had done her job, was about to leave until Joan stopped her. She said, "No, don't go; stay with us."

The three of them made love like old times. After they were finished, they lay in the bed enjoying each other's company.

The chatter became more prominent as Miriam struggled to open her eyes. It was the children having breakfast. When Miriam did open her eyes, she was in bed alone. **She had not made love with Joan and Andrew last night. It was all a dream.**

Chapter Eight

The Early Years
Chicago Bound

It wasn't long after Miriam's trial that Audrey also had to face a jury but not for the reason in Miriam's dream. Audrey was indicted for manslaughter in the death of her stepfather. Audrey had killed him, but not because she felt that he was responsible for the death of her mother. She killed because he seemed to have had similar plans for her.

Audrey had tolerated the whippings and abuse from her stepfather after her mother's death, but she wasn't willing to tolerate being his sex thing too. When he made it obvious that he intended for her to take her mother's place, she pushed his sorry ass down the stairs. He died from the tumble, and a broken neck.

The police had looked for Audrey to question her in the matter, but her whereabouts was unknown. The District Attorney in Chicago saw Audrey's picture when it was shown on national news during Miriam's trial.

Because Audrey's trial was to take place in Chicago, Andrew, Audrey and the children moved back to the windy city. The trial

Chicago Bound

was expected to take about a month, so Andrew and his family, once again, took up residence in Luke's big house.

The size of Andrew's family increased when he returned to his hometown. That's when he met his fourth son for the first time. Eugene's mother, Gina, only told Andrew about his son when she was beset by medical problems that made her unable to take care of Eugene. With the help of a nanny, Luke took care of his grandson when Gina was hospitalized for cancer treatment. Gina pleaded with Andrew to take care of their son, knowing that she was dying.

The fact that Gina was dying reminded Andrew how sudden death can be. He remembered having a loving mother one day and the next day she was gone.

Andrew and Audrey's marriage was still in trouble when they moved back to Chicago. They hadn't made love since Andrew learned of Audrey's past relationship with Miriam. Audrey now felt an even greater urgency to fix things between her and Andrew since new revelations of her past put even greater stress on their marriage.

One day, Audrey had been away from home for much of the day tending to errands. When she returned the nannies had fed the children. They were all now napping except for baby Ann. Andrew was attending to Ann, whose chatter wasn't about to let her fall asleep anytime soon. When baby Ann saw Audrey, her chatter turned to laughter as she squirmed in Andrew's arms and reached for her mother. When Audrey took her daughter, baby Ann tangled her tiny fingers in her mother's hair as if to punish her for having been gone so long.

Luther C. Grayer

As usual, Audrey understood her baby's message. She apologized for having to be away. Baby Ann lessened her grip of her mother's silky hair as if she had accepted her apology and in an instant, she was asleep in her mother's arms.

That was another time that Andrew had witnessed the exceptional communication bond between mother and her child. It was a beautiful thing to see.

Later that evening, now that Audrey had successfully resolved matters with her daughter, who now lay sleeping in her crib, she was ready to continue her ongoing efforts to resolve matters with her husband.

Audrey said, "I love you Andrew."

Andrew, evidently willing to dialog for the moment, coldly replied, "You mean the way you loved Miriam or maybe the way you still love her. Did you two plan all this together?"

"No, we didn't. I did this all on my own. I double-crossed her." Andrew didn't respond, as was the case a lot lately. He would ignore Audrey. Audrey kept talking but this time she unbuttoned her blouse and removed it, and then she said, "Miriam talked about you a lot, and that made me want what she had and what Joan had."

Andrew still didn't speak which prompted Audrey to continue what was becoming a plan. She removed her skirt while repeating her statement. "Miriam talked about you a lot, and that made me want what she had and what Joan had."

The comment about Joan didn't cause Andrew to speak, but it did cause him to look Audrey's way. Audrey then removed the straps of her slip from her shoulders allowing the garment

Chicago Bound

to fall to the floor. She stepped clear of the slip being careful not to get it caught on the stylish three-inch stilettos that she wore. Now wearing nothing but matching panties and bra, bridged by a garter belt that held her stockings in place, she said, "They had everything including a good man and they let you go."

Andrew peered at Audrey and suddenly, as if ashamed of what she was doing, Audrey quickly put on her skirt and blouse. It was good that she had covered up. The nanny entered the room seconds later to report that all the children had been put to bed. The nanny also told Audrey that she had found one of her gold earrings and one of the charms from her bracelet in Crystal's pocket. The nanny said while smiling, "Even at three years old, she's such a lady. She loves shiny jewelry already."

After the nanny had left, Audrey only had a second to contemplate how her charm had gotten to Miriam's apartment. Crystal had taken it there.

Andrew now apparently ready to dialog more said, with no preamble, "You don't want what Joan has. That woman is out of her mind."

Audrey had to get up to speed. Andrew was responding to the statement that she had made before the nanny came into the room. Audrey was good, she was back on track in no time. "You're right Andrew. I don't want to be sick like Joan was, but I wanted everything else she had."

Andrew continued to speak negatively about his ex-wife, but he spoke with passion. He then asked Audrey what she had meant when she said that she had double-crossed Miriam.

Audrey took a deep breath and said, "Miriam was working to get you and Joan back together, but I stepped into the picture before she could work that out."

"What do you mean? Miriam is the one who convinced Joan to leave me in the first place, and then she convinced her to divorce me. Miriam is looking out for herself and nobody else."

Suddenly with tears in her eyes, Audrey said, "I'm afraid of going to jail. I don't want to be away from our baby. Don't give up on me Andrew."

Audrey knew that Andrew would never give up on her in that way. He would use the necessary resources to get her off. She only said it because she didn't want him to give up on her as a wife, something he was on the verge of doing.

Women are good. They're smart. They know the right strings to pull, and exactly when to pull them. At that moment, Audrey decided to go for it all, she said, "Send me away if you want to, Andrew, but I'm not going to leave unless you tell me you don't love me anymore. You told me that once before and you didn't mean it then. Can you tell me that you don't love me now, Andrew?"

Andrew hesitated, and then he simply said, "No. I can't."

Audrey had played her hand just right, having felt that Andrew wouldn't be able to say that he didn't love her. He didn't have to tell her that he loved her at that moment. She knew that in time he would say those words again.

As if it was an after thought, Andrew suddenly said, "What was all that undressing about?"

Audrey, while blushing, said in a long drawn out manner,

Chicago Bound

"Oh-h-h-h-h-h I don't know-w-w-w-w-w. I guess I just wanted to get your attention."

"You got my attention," and then he said, "Get my attention again."

Audrey took Andrew's hand and led him to their bedroom. She became his dirty dancer that night. They talked a lot more, but more importantly, they made love. It was the start of good times again.

Audrey had the best defense team that money could buy. Her trial only took two weeks instead of the month that was anticipated. The court ruled that she had acted in self-defense when she pushed her stepfather, Mr. Crum, down the stairs. The testimony of witnesses attesting to his brutality toward Audrey's mother and other women made a strong case for the defense.

Mr. Crum was shown to be a sorry excuse for a man, spending time in jail for domestic battery on many occasions. Audrey's testimony that her being fourteen at the time, she was afraid to leave. Her stepfather had threatened to find her and do to her what he had done to her mother. That night as Crum tried to pull Audrey into his room, they struggled at the top of the stairs, and that's when it happened. She pushed him while trying to get away. The jury had no problem with deciding this case.

After the trial, Andrew and Audrey decided not to return to Boston choosing instead to remain in Chicago where they grew up. Andrew didn't realize how much he had missed being around his large family.

The big house was full again. Luke and his girlfriend moved out completely, leaving the house to Andrew and his immediate family, which was to become even larger.

Luther C. Grayer

Andrew moved Gina into Victoria's wing of the house so that she could spend as much time with their son as possible. Joan and Miriam remained in Boston to continue college. They didn't object to the kids living in Chicago with Andrew, since they had to devote so much time to their studies. In the beginning, Joan and Miriam would see the kids two or three times a month, flying to Chicago on weekends and staying at the big house. There was a lot of travel involved, but they made it work. During summer break, travel was less, since they would be with the kids for at least a month at a time.

It was a unique situation to say the least when the four women that bore Andrew's children were all in the same house at once. Audrey was gracious sharing her home with the women that had been Andrew's lovers. The saying that it takes a village to raise a child was paramount in Audrey's mind. She wanted what was best for the children. Audrey was sharing her home, but she wasn't sharing her husband. She simply told Andrew no messing around.

Gina became especially close to Miriam. Maybe it was because Gina felt guilty that Miriam had to endure two trials for a murder that Gina knew she didn't commit.

Joan and Miriam's relationship started to fall apart a few months after Miriam's trial. Audrey was the first person that Miriam had cheated with but she wasn't the last. Miriam needed variety so she cheated on Joan again. Joan didn't take it though. She put Miriam out so that she could be free to pursue love where ever and with whomever she wanted. Miriam eventually left Boston for destinations unknown. She left more than Joan behind. She left her son, Austin, as well. If you are going to lose your mother, perhaps four was not a bad age, especially if there were substitute mothers around. Joan had been there from the beginning and continued to love Austin as if he had come from her body.

A year after Miriam had left her son, Gina left her son as well. It wasn't by choice though. Gina fought the good fight but passed on two years after being diagnosed with cancer. Audrey became a substitute mom to Eugene, who was fourteen months older than her daughter, Ann.

Joan finished her second year of dental school and transferred to The University of Illinois at Chicago. She wanted to be around her children more now that she had gotten much of her schooling out of the way. Her children were just starting their schooling and she didn't want to miss that. A.J. was seven and entering second grade, while Austin and the twins were starting kindergarten. That was also around the time when Joan realized that she still loved Andrew but understood that she had caused him to turn to other women and that Andrew now had a wife that he loved very much.

Joan was going to live on the university's campus, but Audrey and Andrew thought that it would be a good idea that she move into Victoria's wing of the big house. With Joan living there, she could help more with the children, which would be a good thing since Audrey was expecting again. Andrew was going to be a father for the seventh time. That meant that he would at least equal his father in the number of offspring produced.

Joan and Audrey didn't know each other very well despite their frequent contact during the years that Audrey had been married to Andrew. Their relationship began because they were raising children who had the same father. Joan and Audrey became good friends during the next few months. Although Joan was busy with classes, she was a great comfort to Audrey during the first eight months of her pregnancy. It was a difficult pregnancy. The baby threatened to be born prematurely several times, but each time doctors were able to slow the process and keep things on track.

During Joan's spring break, she and Audrey spent most of their days together supervising the children and talking about what they wanted for them. They even made a pact that if anything were to happen to either of them, the other would take care of their children. One day they sat talking. While rubbing her stomach, Audrey said, "I want to name this baby Drew for Andrew." They had already learned the baby's sex and Andrew didn't like the name Drew for a girl.

Joan said, "I like it. I'm sure Andrew will come around."

As Joan finished her statement, Audrey's labor pains started. Everything was ready. Andrew had been prepared for weeks. He was ready for his daughter to be born. Andrew and Audrey were about to leave for the hospital when baby Ann started to cry. Joan picked Ann up and caressed her to stop her from crying. Joan's soothing touch did the trick. She told Audrey that she would take care of her until she returned. Joan took a seat in the rocker and watched from the window as Andrew and Audrey pulled out of the driveway.

The nanny put baby Ann to bed minutes later, after she had fallen asleep in Joan's arms. Joan then fell asleep herself and her future appeared.

Chicago Bound

After Audrey had her baby, she and Joan became even closer as friends. Audrey even registered for classes; she too wanted to have a career one day. Both Joan and Audrey recognized the danger of them being attracted to each other, but they were more excited about the danger than they were worried about it.

After one of their study sessions, Audrey sat in what was now Joan's apartment listening at Andrew's blaring horn signaling her to come out. They were supposed to be going to a movie. Joan said while looking out the window, "Andrew is blowing for you."

Audrey said, "I know" and continued to sit comfortably with her arms folded.

After a few minutes of intermittent horn blowing, Andrew made his way to the door. As Joan walked across the room to open the door, she said, "Your husband is going to be angry at you for making him come in to get you."

Audrey said, "You might be right. Let me get the door."

When Audrey opened the door, Andrew, with mild irritation, asked, "Didn't you hear me blowing? We're going to be late."

Audrey said, "I'm sorry, baby," as she closed the door, then she kissed Andrew and grinded on him. Joan stood in shock watching. Now embarrassed she turned to leave. Audrey said, "No, don't go. Come help me." This was like something that had happened before, but this time it was Joan who was being given permission to partake of Andrew.

Andrew pulled away from Audrey, but didn't offer much resistance. While still grinding on Andrew, Audrey beckoned to Joan and said again, "Come help me, Joan.

115

Joan was reluctant to participate, but she did respond to Audrey's invitation. When Joan reached the couple, Audrey still had the quarry in her grasp, Audrey put one arm around Joan while encircling Andrew with her other arm causing them to create a circle. Audrey then wedged Joan between Andrew and her. Joan now stood facing Andrew while her backside was the recipient of Audrey's rhythmic rotating hips. The three of them now participated in gyrations that caused heat. Andrew, now sufficiently mesmerized, followed when Audrey led Joan to the bedroom. They made love as a threesome for the first time that day.

The sound of the phone caused Joan to awake. **That's when she realized that the three of them hadn't made love; it was all a dream.**

Andrew had called to say he and Audrey had arrived at the hospital. After Audrey was examined, it was determined that her baby was experiencing problems. They had to get her to the delivery room immediately. Andrew was to go into the delivery room too, but the doctor asked that he not, since the baby was experiencing problems.

As they wheeled Audrey away with Andrew walking along side, Audrey said, "Smile, baby. I'm about to give you another daughter."

Andrew did smile, but it was for Audrey's sake. He was worried. This baby was having problems early on and she was still having problems. Andrew's last words to Audrey were, "I love you, Audrey." He had said that to her a lot during the last couple of years just as Audrey had predicted he would.

Chicago Bound

It was more than two hours before the doctor finished. From the look on his face, as he approached Andrew, Andrew knew that his daughter didn't make it. Confirmation of Andrew's suspicions came when the doctor said, "I'm sorry we couldn't save her."

Andrew was sad but he was prepared since the baby had been experiencing problems from the beginning. The doctor realized he had made a mistake even before Andrew asked, "How's my wife taking it?"

This time the doctor's words pierced Andrew's soul like none had ever before. He fell to his knees when the doctor said, "I'm so sorry, Mr. Grant," he paused, as if trying to find a softer way to deliver a hard blow. "It's your wife who didn't make it."

The doctor's words continued to rattle in Andrew's brain with such force that they threatened to cause his head to explode. Andrew had to be admitted to the hospital and was unable to leave for two days. Luke and other family members took Andrew home. He had to learn how to go on, after the death of a woman he loved. Something his father, Luke, has had do a number of times.

Chapter Nine

The Early Years
Metamorphosis

Andrew became a bitter man after Audrey's death. It was as if he didn't like anybody. He drowned himself in sex, having lots of partners, but they were professionals. Andrew paid for sexual services because he wasn't taking any chances on anybody getting pregnant or anybody falling in love. He knew that neither would happen with these high price girls.

Joan tried to help Andrew as a concerned mother not as a woman wanting him as a man. She wanted Andrew at his best for the children. Joan loved him, but felt guilty for entertaining the thought that since Audrey was gone she could now step back into his life. She did quit school having to take total responsibility for the children now that she was the only parent available. Andrew, with his active sex life, just didn't deal with them.

A year after Audrey's death, Andrew was still in bad shape. Joan had overcome her reluctance to try for a come back. Luke had convinced her that it wasn't wrong for her to love Andrew and to want him back. Joan actively pursued Andrew, but he wasn't interested, and one night, after having enough to drink, he was going to prove it. Andrew brought one of his high paid companions home. She was beautiful having a long lean body that rivaled that of any super model. As they sat on the couch, the noise they made awoke Joan and even the children. There was chaos to say the least. Ann and baby Drew were in their cribs crying. They were frightened. Joan made her way to the living room, where Andrew, in a drunken manner, was assuring his companion that everything was fine.

"This is my house. They'll go back to sleep."

By this time, the five older children had made their way to the living room. They were now surrounding Joan, tugging at her robe, as if seeking safety from some monster that had invaded their sleep.

Noticing them all hovering around, Andrew yelled, "You kids go to bed. What're you doing up anyway?"

Joan quickly dispatched the children to the girls' room telling A.J. to take Eugene's hand and go check on baby Drew. She told Austin, Christian and Crystal to check on Ann. The nanny was already in the room with the two youngest. This was Joan's way of limiting the older children's exposure to their father at a time when he was at his worse.

Andrew's companion had been drinking, too, but not nearly as much as Andrew. Her assessment of the situation led her to apologize. She said Joan, "I didn't know that he was bringing me to the house where his wife and children lived."

Andrew nearly asleep now said in a drunken manner, "No, that's not my wife. I don't have a wife." Andrew's companion continued to apologize while she moved toward the door.

Andrew continued his plea, but he was almost out. He said, "Don't go, Joy. Your name is Joy, right?" And, with that, Andrew was out like a blown light bulb.

Joy was at the door now, but before she could open it, Joan asked, "Did you drive?"

"I drove us in his car."

Joan, pointing to the phone insisted that Joy call a cab. While Joy summoned a cab, Joan went through Andrew's pockets, as he was now sound asleep. Joan asked, "How much does he owe you?"

"No, he paid me for the whole night." Then, as if to make up for the wrong she felt, Joy asked, "Do you want part of it back? We didn't do anything."

"No, you keep it. Here's money for the cab." Joan gave her two of the fifty-dollar bills that she had taken from Andrew's pocket.

The next morning as the children were finishing breakfast, the chatter was loud as they toyed with each other. Sometime the activity progressed to the point that Joan or one of the nannies had to step in to calm things down. When Andrew entered the room, all chatter stopped. Ann and Drew's activity stopped too, puzzled by the sudden inactivity of their older brothers and sister. Andrew didn't stay long. He spoke and got himself a cup of coffee and continued on to the den. A.J. asked his mother, "When's dad going to be alright again?"

"I don't know, baby, but I hope soon." She then told the nannies that they could take the children outside for play.

When Joan entered the den, Andrew was sitting staring out the window. He could see the children playing. "I want to take the children away for a while Andrew, until you get better."

Metamorphosis

"I'm fine, and you're not taking the children anywhere. They're not your children anyway."

Andrew's statement brought tears to Joan's eyes. She sobbed, "Three of them are mine Andrew and I love them all as if they were mine."

"Well you can't take them and I'll use all my resources to see to that."

Joan had never seen this side of Andrew before, and she didn't want to see more. She didn't say anymore about taking the children for fear that Andrew might use his father's empire to wage war on her. Even though Joan was finished, Andrew wasn't. He said, "I'll let you and the kids stay here though. I'm moving out."

Joan was relieved since it would've been difficult for her to find a place large enough for them all. "Okay," she said. "That's best anyway, with everything already set-up here I can start back to school next term."

Joan was shocked when Andrew sarcastically asked, "Where's your school money going to come from?"

Joan didn't answer Andrew's question which she knew was only asked rhetorically anyway. He was telling her that he wasn't paying for her school anymore. If it wasn't clear before, it was now. Andrew intended to punish her, maybe even make her beg. Their conversation was interrupted by the sound of baby Drew's cry. When the nanny entered the room carrying the baby she said, "She has a fever."

Joan said, "Give her to me and call the doctor." The doctor gave Joan instructions and told her to bring the baby in if the fever wasn't down in an hour. Drew's temperature was back to normal within forty minutes and she was her happy self again. Joan spent the rest of the day with the children, and Andrew left for his evening festivities.

We all have seen or read of those who have lost the love of their life. Some of us are losers ourselves. The pain is often more than one could bear and the loser sometimes succumbed to a faith of demise too. In most cases though, we don't fall victim to that degree. We carried on instead. It's usually with the help of others or our responsibilities to others that causes us to move forward. In Andrew's case, both factors were there. His family offered him support and his children needed his parenting. To this day though, those factors hadn't been enough to put Andrew on the right track.

One day, while Luke was visiting his grandchildren, he could feel Joan's sadness. She was no longer in school pursuing the education that she always wanted. When Luke asked why she was no longer in school, she answered, "I'm tired and just want to spend more time with the childrew."

Luke knew it was the kind of answer a person gave when they couldn't tell the truth. "How are things with you and Andrew since you told him how you felt?"

Once again, Joan's answer wasn't the truth. She said, "We're working things out dad."

Luke knew it wasn't true. He understood that it was difficult for Joan to talk negatively about Andrew to him. It's different with children though. They were old enough to see what was happening, yet young enough to tell the truth. Kids are innocent that way, or they're smarter than we think.

Metamorphosis

Luke was sitting with Christian at his little desk. Christian, showing his grandfather his first grade school work, said, "Dad doesn't look at my work the way he used to look at my brother A.J.'s work."

"Why do you think that is, Christian?"

"I don't know, Grandpa. He might be too busy with his friends now. He brought one home one night. She was tall and her skirt was real short. Daddy yelled at us that night to go back to bed!" Then Christian laid his head on his desk and said, "My daddy made my mommy cry that night. Mommy cries a lot now."

That night when all was quiet, four brothers lay in their beds talking. A.J. said, "Christian you did real well today with grandpa."

Christian feeling proud that he had his big brother's stamp of approval said, "Thanks A.J."

A.J. then said to Austin, "It'll be your turn next."

Austin said, "I'll be ready. But do you think this is going to help mom?"

A.J. said, "For sure. Grandpa can fix anything. He'll make Dad alright again."

Eugene, who was just four said, "I want a turn too."

Over the next few days, Eugene and all the other children had a turn. A.J., with all of his eight years of wisdom, managed to orchestrate events that innocently gave Luke a picture of what was happening at home. A.J. managed to get his grandfather to come to the house regularly the next two weeks and on each occasion, Luke would get some idea of his son's family life.

Luke had a theory. Actually, he had many theories, but this one pertained to love, and why love became hate. In Luke's mind, one sure way to cause love to become hate was to deny someone their dream out of spite. As a parent, Luke tried to stay out of his grown children's affairs but not to a point that he would allow their demise. Luke had to interfere to help set his son right.

In business, Luke was always able to analyze his problems and formulate strategies to solve them. He was not prone to indecisiveness nor was he one who second-guessed himself once a decision was made. His multi-million dollar company would not have been built if tough decisions weren't made and seen through. When it came to making decisions concerning his children, it was different. He wasn't dealing with money. He was dealing with the lives of people he loved.

Luke had decided that in order to save his son he had to save Joan first, and like parents everywhere, who make decisions which affect their children, he prayed that it was a good decision.

It took a couple of days for the attorney to draw up the documents that Luke had requested. When Luke got to the big house that he had owned for nearly thirty years, his four older grandchildren were still at school and the three younger children were napping. Luke had planned it that way so that he and Joan could talk undisturbed. As Luke stood at the front door waiting to be let in, a flood of memories invaded his mind. When Mildred, Luke's housekeeper for thirty years, opened the door, she registered surprise and said, "Oh, Mr. Grant, Hi. Your grandchildren didn't get home yet."

"Hi, Mildred; I'm not here to see the kids now. I'll see them later. Tell Joan that I'm here and then you join us in the den."

Luke laid out the documents that his lawyer had prepared along with three pens. The documents were a series of legal papers setting up trust funds for Luke's seven grandchildren. Joan was made executor of the funds and allocated compensation for her services. Luke also gave his big house to his seven grandchildren and once again made Joan executor, with live-in privileges until the youngest child becomes an adult.

Mildred signed each document as a witness to Luke and Joan's signatures. Each time Joan signed one of the documents, tears welled in her eyes. By the time she had signed the last document, the wells of her eyes weren't enough to hold the tears. They ran down her face as if floodgates had been opened.

Baby Drew was sixteen months old now, and Joan felt comfortable leaving her home with the nannies. The nannies had been with the family since before Ann was born and Joan trusted them to take good care of the children in her absence.

Now that she had money, Joan enrolled in school again. She had one more year of dental studies to complete. Her fourth day of classes was the first time she noticed Jerry but it wasn't the first time he had noticed her. Jerry was extremely handsome and when he approached Joan and asked if they could have coffee after class, she was tempted to say yes, but she said no. After all, she had children waiting for her at home.

During the next two weeks, Jerry continued to show interest in Joan, and Joan continued rejecting his offers. Joan eventually told Jerry that she was responsible for seven children, who kelp her busy.

One morning before class, Joan was sitting in the cafeteria having finished her coffee but still struggling to finish her assignment. She had missed a part of yesterday's lecture because of a flat tire, and whatever she had missed was proving to be essential for completing the assignment.

When Jerry spoke to Joan, she looked at him as if he was a lifesaver. She said, "I was hoping someone would be here early enough who could help me with this assignment."

Jerry jokingly said, "Sure, anything for a price." Before Joan could respond, Jerry said, "Just kidding. Let's see where you are." When Jerry examined Joan's work he saw that she was meticulous, but she was missing a step in measuring the length of a nerve in one of the canals of a tooth in need of a root canal. After having explained the missing step, Joan was able to finish her assignment in almost no time.

There was still had twenty minutes before class and Joan couldn't pretend to work on her assignment since Jerry was as smart as she was and knew that the assignment was complete.

Jerry asked, "How many of those seven children are yours?"

Joan answered Jerry's question with a question. "You don't think that I could have seven children?"

"No. Not at your age and be in the last year of dental school too." Joan never answered the question, but they did continue to talk until the bell for the first class rung.

During the next week, Joan and Jerry worked on several projects together. One evening after finishing their work, Joan accepted Jerry's offer for dinner. She didn't know whether it was because she was hungry or because she was hoping that Jerry could convince her to sleep with him. Whatever the reason, Joan

Metamorphosis

went on a date with a man other than Andrew for first time in over ten years.

When Jerry, being the gentleman that he was, held the door for Joan, her fragrance was mesmerizing as she glided past him. Joan had freshened up having a change of essentials in her gym locker. During dinner, it took all of Jerry's strength to resist taking this beautiful woman in his arms and smothering her with kisses.

After dinner, Jerry escorted Joan to her car and could no longer resist touching her. As Joan fumbled to unlock the driver side door to her car, which the remote didn't activate, Jerry moved closer to assist causing his front side to make contact with Joan's backside. Their bodies merged causing Jerry's manhood to stiffen. Feeling Jerry's hardness caused Joan's body to respond with subtle gyrations only detectable by Jerry. Jerry encircled Joan with both arms squeezing her tight while kissing her on the neck. Their passionate moment was interrupted by the ring of Joan's cell phone. It was her daughter Crystal, who was expecting her mother earlier. Joan was to help her daughter with some schoolwork.

Joan said to Jerry, "Sorry. I told you I had seven children."

As Joan drove off, Jerry said out loud, "Yes, you did."

Joan was surprised the next day when Jerry offered to fix her dinner while they worked on the latest assignment. She asked, "Why are you interested in a woman who has had three children and is responsible for four others?"

Jerry didn't answer Joan's question, or maybe he did. He said, "You are so beautiful!" Jerry's words and the way he looked at Joan caused her to quiver. The thought of being held by a man again was causing something within her to stir. With some reluctance, Joan accepted Jerry's offer.

That evening at Jerry's apartment, it didn't take long for Jerry to pick up where he had left off yesterday. No sooner than the door to the apartment was closed, Jerry encircled Joan with both arms but this time they were facing each other. Jerry massaged Joan's backside causing her dress to rise, exposing her panties. Jerry lowered the panties to Joan's knees exposing her hairy jewel. When Jerry touched Joan there, she went limp, almost sagging to the floor. Jerry picked Joan up with her panties still around her knees. He carried her to the bed and finished removing the panties along with Joan's shoes. She now lay naked from the waist down. Jerry proceeded to finish the pleasurable task of undressing her.

Now completely exposed, Joan attempted to pull the covers over her, but Jerry would have none of that. He pulled the covers back, insisting on enjoying the view. Joan said in a babyish way, "Not fair. You've got your clothes on."

"That's not my fault," said Jerry.

Joan moved to the edge of the bed and stood up. She began to undress Jerry. She kissed him on the lips and once his chest was exposed, she kissed it. Joan kneeled down to untie Jerry's shoes. She then guided him to the edge of the bed and gently pushed him to a sitting position, and then she removed his pants. Jerry was now wearing nothing but his jockey shorts, which were restraining his bulging manhood. Joan playfully toyed with releasing Jerry's manhood, as if she was afraid that it would get her. When Joan

Metamorphosis

did remove Jerry's shorts, his manhood sprung free with a mighty force. They made love for a good portion of the evening. Jerry was only the second man to take Joan's sex.

During the next few months, life for Joan continued to be good. She was nearing graduation and she had a boyfriend that she enjoyed having sex with. Even though seven children caused time restraints that didn't allow Joan to spend as much time with Jerry as either of them wanted, they were making the best of things.

Joan's relations with Andrew's family grew stronger. She spent more time with them now than Andrew did. Joan became especially close to Grace, one of Andrew's nieces. Joan was only a few years older than Grace, but Grace admired Joan and looked to her as a role model. Grace, who was in her second year of college, changed her major to a pre-dental curriculum. She wanted to be like Joan.

One day after Joan and Jerry had made love, they lay in bed talking. Joan said, "I've got to go. My baby has a cold."

Jerry in a disappointed manner said, "Which of your babies is it this time?" Jerry wanted Joan to stay so that they could take another trip through Loveland.

Joan could sense that Jerry was upset. She said, "Drew has a cold and I promised to be home early."

"There are three adults home with your baby. They can take care of a little cold." Joan had started dressing but was having trouble locating her bra. As she stood there in just her panties, she looked as good as ever. Jerry said, "Come back to bed, baby. I'll get you home."

Luther C. Grayer

Joan was torn between her womanly desires to be with a man that she enjoyed having sex with, and her motherly instincts to take care of the child that she loved as her own.

She said in a way that indicated her regret, "No, Jerry. I've got to go." This wasn't the first time that motherly instincts had won out. Jerry had been disappointed before.

Sometimes life was cruel, but there were times when it seemed worse than that. Everybody took it hard when Audrey died giving birth to Drew two years ago, and now, they had to suffer the death of baby Drew, too.

It happened suddenly. Drew didn't wake up one morning. The autopsy showed that her brain was lacking sufficient oxygen to function. Joan took the death hard, blaming herself for being too busy to notice that something was wrong. Joan dropped out of school, again, and stopped seeing Jerry. It was as if she wasn't going to let anything get in the way of her looking after the children from now on.

Andrew's plight was different. He was still grieving the death of Audrey, which had caused him to spiral out of control, but the death of baby Drew caused an awakening that saved him from self-destruction. Andrew grieved over the loss of his daughter but strangely, it made him grateful for the six children he had, and he wanted to be a part of their lives again.

During this time, Andrew had another revelation. He realized that he was still in love with the woman he'd loved from the first moment he met her. Andrew now knew that he had been angry with Joan because she allowed him to fall in love with someone else, while he still loved her. Loving two women and feeling guilty for it was a difficult place to be, which was where Andrew had been for a time in his life.

Andrew worked hard to help Joan through her bad time. He didn't try anything sexual; he just wanted Joan to be all right again. He was even willing to see her with Jerry if that would make her better. One day as they sat talking, Andrew said, "I saw Jerry this morning. I told him to come for lunch tomorrow. I'm going to be away all day."

Joan reacted as if insulted; with her hands on her hips, she said, "You did what? I don't need you to be my pimp Andrew. I can get a man if I want one." Joan then showed off what truly was a beautiful physique. "Does this look like I need your help to get a man?"

"No you can get any man you want." Andrew continued as if embarrassed for having said the wrong thing. "I'm sorry Joan; I thought that's what you wanted."

"Jerry's a good man. He deserves a woman with a lot less baggage than I've got. He needs a woman who can give him his own babies." Joan realized that Jerry was not the man for her. Then she said, "You're trying to give me to another man. I remember you once cried when you thought of me with another man."

Andrew said, "The last thing that I would ever want to do is give you away, but I know that I've been such a fool." Suddenly Andrew decided to go for it all. He said, in a manly way, "I don't want you to ever sleep with anybody else as long as I live." Andrew held his breath waiting for Joan to put him in his place. He was ready for the worst, but he didn't know that Joan's response would make him cry.

She simply, "Okay," and then she added, "But that means that you can' sleep with anybody else either."

Who says a man's not supposed to cry? Sometimes men get it right too. Andrew knew the right string to pull and he knew when to pull it. He had done well and now had another chance with the woman he loved.

Andrew thought, in silence, *what a wise man my father is*. Luke knew that anger often manifests itself as hate. He didn't allow Andrew to punish Joan by depriving her of her dream. That would have caused her love to turn to hate and hate never turns back to love again.

Joan and Andrew were married a second time. Andrew started his college career after that. Even though he would inherit a fortune one day, he wanted to earn a living. Not only did Andrew want Joan's love, he wanted her respect too.

Chapter Ten

The Gathering
The Story Returns to the Present Day. We Continue with Joan and Andrew on the Golf Course.

After Joan and Andrew had finished the first nine holes of their Saturday round of golf, they had a quick repast and proceeded to the tenth tee. While playing his second nine of the golf, Andrew made some mistakes; but he was perfect on the last hole. He stepped to the tee and hit his drive long and straight down the middle of the fairway; the perfect drive allowed Andrew to eagle the eighteenth hole.

For those who don't know golf, an eagle is quite a feat; it's like a three run homer in baseball. In life Andrew made mistakes, too, but he made a lot of eagles as well.

Later that evening, Joan and Andrew had dinner at their favorite restaurant. That night as Joan drove them home, she complimented Andrew on how well he played the eighteenth hole earlier that day.

"It's the toughest hole on the golf course," she said, "and you handled it well." As they were pulling into the driveway Joan said, "Now mister; you have some other business to handle." Andrew leaned over and kissed Joan on the lips, as he looked forward to the rest of the evening and handling his business.

The next morning, Andrew awoke when he heard Joan say, "Wake up, baby." Andrew was about to get excited, thinking Joan was going to treat him to another trip through Loveland, that is until she said, "We need to leave for the airport in five minutes."

It was six o'clock Sunday morning and Andrew only now remembered that they had to pick up Angela and Walter from the airport.

The plane was on time, and after the two couples found each other, they headed home for breakfast. As they entered the house, the phone rang; it was A.J.

Andrew and A.J. talked for a while, and at the end of their conversation, A.J. asked to speak to his brother Austin. Andrew gave the phone to Joan, and then he went to get Austin. Austin wasn't in his room. His bed was still made up which meant he hadn't come home last night. When Andrew returned to the phone, he said to A.J., "Your brother is not here. By the way, I thought you were going to spend part of the weekend here."

"I am, Dad; but I won't be there until tomorrow. I'll get Ann and Eugene from the airport on my way."

Andrew said, Okay son, I'll see all my sons tomorrow.

Andrew's use of the word son caused A.J. to think of his son, Andy. As Andrew continued to talk, A.J.'s thoughts to carry him back in time, and he recalled the night that Andy was conceived. It was prom night and Marilyn let A.J. go all the way.

The Gathering

A.J. hadn't even planned to go to the prom until he heard that Marilyn had turned down offers from other boys and made it known, to A.J.'s best friend, that she was hoping that A.J. would ask her. A.J. wasn't so confident a person back then and was surprised that such a beautiful girl wanted him to take her to the prom.

The dance had been a beautiful affair, but the real action started after the dance. Some of the students went to private parties, while others went to expensive restaurants that they only went to with their parents. Others went directly somewhere to make out. A.J. and Marilyn, along with A.J.'s friend, James, and his date went out to eat and ended up at James' house. James lived with his mother, who was away from home a lot. That afforded James a place to bring girls.

The two couples didn't spend much time together once they got to James' house. James took his date to his mother's bedroom leaving his room for A.J. It wasn't a certainty that A.J. was going to score or even that he was going to try, but James set things up for him anyway. He had told A.J. earlier, "When a girl likes you, you make her give it up."

As A.J. and Marilyn sat on the sofa A.J. leaned over and kissed her. He had decided to go for it; James' words resounded in his head. A.J. put his hand under Marilyn's wide bottom dress and felt her warm thighs. She pushed his hand away and said, "No, I can't."

A.J. kissed her again and said, "I just want to touch it."

She didn't push his hand away the second time, but she did say, "We're only going to touch tonight, okay." A.J. massaged

Marilyn's jewel and then he began to remove her panties. She offered resistance but eventually gave up her underwear. A.J.'s manhood was now about to break through his pants. He undid his trousers and told Marilyn to touch it. With reluctance she touched A.J., which made him even harder. Andrew pushed Marilyn to a reclined position and then he lifted her dress so that it covered her head. As he prepared to enter her, she said, "You have a condom don't you?"

"No, but I'm not going to come in you. I'm going to take it out before then."

"Doesn't James have an extra condom?"

"No, he only had one."

This was Marilyn's first time. As A.J. entered her, she said, "Don't come in me, A.J."

A.J. kept his promise; he withdrew, seemingly before coming, but he sprayed Marilyn in the process. She exclaimed, "Ooh, watch where you're shooting that stuff! It's so much. You better not get it on my dress!"

"I'm sorry. I'll get you a towel."

Marilyn soon learned that she should have been worried about more than semen on her dress. She learned a few weeks later that she was pregnant.

Suddenly A.J.'s thoughts returned to the present when he heard his father say, "Son, you're so quiet. Did you fall asleep on me?"

"I'm sorry, Dad; I was thinking about Andy. What did you say?"

"Nothing son, I'll see you tomorrow."

The Gathering

Just as Andrew was about to end the call, Austin entered the house accompanied by a beautiful woman. They were holding hands.

"Wait!" Andrew exclaimed, "Your brother just walked in." Andrew laid the phone down and called out to Austin, "A.J. wants to talk to you."

After the brothers ended the call, Austin introduced his companion to the family. At the end of the introduction, Andrew realized that he had seen Charlene before, but he couldn't remember where.

Andrew invited Austin and Charlene to join them for breakfast."

As Austin was about to respond, Charlene said, "That'll be great. I'm starving."

While they all sat eating and indulging in conversation, Andrew remembered where he had seen Charlene. It was three months ago, but she was with A.J. then. They were holding hands too as they came out of the movie theater. They were gone by the time Andrew could park the car, so A.J. didn't see his father that night.

Seeing Charlene with Austin and having seen her with A.J. caused Andrew to remember when A.J. and Austin were kids growing up. Ever since they were little Austin looked up to A.J. and wanted to be like him. Maybe that's why he wanted things his big brother had. If A.J. had a toy, Austin wanted it or one like it. If A.J. became interested in a sport, Austin did too. A.J. was gracious in sharing with Austin things that he had. Andrew recalled that as a kid Austin even wanted A.J.'s girlfriends.

There was no problem back then though. A.J.'s girlfriends were older and wouldn't consider a baby brother who was at lease three years too young. Andrew wondered if things were different now that his sons were grown.

After breakfast, Austin asked his father if Charlene could spend the rest of the weekend. He said, "She could share the room with Crystal and Ann."

"I'm sure that'll be fine with the girls. It's okay with me." That's the thing about a large family, there's always room for one more. Then Andrew, along with Joan, Angela and Walter left for the golf course leaving Austin and Charlene to settle in.

Golf went well; the whole day did, but now Andrew was exhausted from activities that had started at six that morning. When they returned home, it was nearly eleven o'clock, and Austin and Charlene were probably in bed, since Austin's car was still in the driveway. Andrew was ready for bed himself. He excused himself from the others and after a fitting goodnight kiss from Joan, he headed for the bedroom. Before Andrew could get to his room, Austin came out of the girl's bedroom. He said, "Dad. I was just saying goodnight to Charlene."

"Okay. Is everything alright?"

"Yes; everything's fine, Dad." Austin then headed to his bedroom.

With a grin meant only for himself, Andrew thought *all the children will be here tomorrow. That'll keep him in the right bedroom.*

Angela wasn't far behind Andrew in her retreat to the solitude of the guest bedroom. That left Joan and Walter alone to catch up on brother-sister stuff.

The Gathering

Andrew was asleep within a minute of getting into bed; his sleep was interrupted five hours later as Joan was just coming to bed. She and Walter had talked all night. Peering at the illuminated clock and struggling to suppress a yawn, Andrew asked, "Have you been up all this time?"

"I'm sorry I woke you, go back to sleep. Go to sleep, baby"

Andrew didn't have any trouble doing what Joan said. He was asleep within thirty seconds. Joan was unable to take her own advice though, as she lay in bed unable to fall asleep. her talk with her brother had her mind working overtime. Joan's thoughts carried her back in time; she recalled the day that Walter and Angela got married.

It was at the wedding that Joan learned that her baby brother, who was then nineteen, was more into drugs than she knew. He had been smoking reefer since he was thirteen, but everybody did; didn't they? Joan having asked herself that question had to laugh since she had never indulged, but she considered herself a square who didn't count. Then she thought Walter didn't indulge either, nor did Andrew and there was nothing square about them at all.

Joan recalled that at her own wedding Andrew went ballistic when he caught Richard offering his niece, a drag on a joint. When Walter learned what had happened, he joined in the ruckus. Joan's thoughts of the past were interrupted when Andrew turned over and touched her. It happened a lot like that in the morning hours. Andrew was ready for lovemaking.

The next morning, Andrew awoke with his normal morning spunk, but not Joan. She didn't even budge when Andrew kissed her on the cheek. She was out for the count. When Andrew entered the living room, he saw Walter asleep on the couch. Before Andrew could decide whether to wake him or not, Walter mumbled, while still half-asleep, "What time is it?"

"It is seven o'clock, brother." Then with a big grin on his face he added, "Man I made love to your sister this morning!" Andrew's grin grew even bigger when he said, "It doesn't look like you made love to my sister though."

Walter, while yawning, said, "You're right, brother, but only because I fell asleep on this couch."

Andrew took a seat next to Walter, who had now assumed a sitting position. In a serious tone, and no longer flashing the grin, Andrew said, "You know, I thought of him as my brother too, and I wish we could have saved him."

They had been trying to save Richard since Andrew caught him smoking pot at his first wedding more than twenty years ago. That day Andrew whipped Richard as if he was Richard's daddy. Richard was no more than twelve at the time and when he told his big brother, Walter, what Andrew had done to him, Andrew thought he would have to fight Walter too. Walter surprised both Andrew and Richard when he asked, "Which cheek of that ass did you get? I'm going to get the other one when we get home." They had waged an ongoing battle since then to free Richard from his demons.

Andrew recalled that a friend of his, who was deep into religion, gave him comfort when Andrew lost his mother. Andrew's friend, with his eyes peering upward to the heavens, said, "you have to know that there is a God who said it was time

The Gathering

for your mother to come home to rest." Andrew told Walter that he needed to believe that there was a God who knew it was time for Richard to come home and rest from his troubles.

Walter wanted to believe; it would make accepting the pain easier knowing that things were being controlled by an all-knowing God. He thought to himself, not wanting to question Andrew, *why did God wait until He had no choice but to take Richard? Why didn't God do something before it was too late?* Andrew and Walter's conversation was interrupted when Angela entered the room.

Like her brother, Angela had gotten a full night's sleep and was ready for the day's activities, but Walter was able to convince his wife to go back to bed with him for the activity that he was now ready for. As they departed for their bedroom, Walter flashed Andrew a grin that meant, I'm about to make love to your sister now. It was a part of the game the brother-in-laws played.

The aroma of coffee drew Andrew to the kitchen. Charlene had brewed a pot and was having a cup. When she saw Andrew, she asked, "Was it okay that I made coffee?"

"Of course it's okay; you can fix anything you want."

"Thank you. I just needed a cup of coffee." Charlene then said, "I think I'll go back to bed if that's okay."

As she was leaving with her coffee in hand, she blurted out with tears running down her face, "I'm pregnant with your grandchild, but I don't know which one of your sons is the father." There was a period of silence. Andrew didn't know how to respond. "You must think that I'm a filthy whore sleeping with brothers."

"No. I don't think that, but I do think that you shouldn't drink a lot of coffee while pregnant." Andrew took the cup from Charlene's hand and said, "Let me fix you some warm milk. My wife liked that when she was pregnant."

Charlene and Andrew talked for more than an hour after which Charlene was ready for a nap. She asked again, "Is it okay if I go back to bed for a while?"

"Of course it is. I'll see you later."

Charlene left for the bedroom and Andrew finished the last of the coffee. Andrew then showered and dressed.

It had been over two hours since Angela was coerced back to bed by her husband, but she was now showered and dressed too, so she and Andrew decided to play golf while their mates slept. On their way out of the driveway, Andrew noticed that Austin's car was gone. Andrew said Angela, "I didn't hear Austin leave this morning."

Angela said, "No. He left last night after you went to bed."

"You mean he left without Charlene?"

"Yes. He said she wasn't feeling well."

It was nearly noon when Joan awoke, following her all night talk session with Walter. Walter also was now awake. He and Angela were scheduled to leave for the airport later that evening. It was just past noon and Joan and Walter had breakfast, as they continued their talk from last night. It was clear that Walter was still suffering. Everybody tried to convince him that he had done all he could to help his brother, but Walter couldn't be convinced of that. In his mind there had to be something else he could have done.

The Gathering

Suddenly Walter said, as if a light just turned on in his brain, "That's it. That's what I should have done."

Joan was startled since there had been a pause in their conversation until Walter's sudden outburst.

She asked, "What should you have done?"

"I should have talked more to you and to anybody else who loved him. Every time he slipped, I should have publicized it, so that he would get a dose of help at every turn from anybody who knew him."

Walter quietly cried, as he often did when he thought of his brother and wished for another chance to do more. As Joan and Walter were finishing their breakfast, Austin came in.

Austin was just getting in from last night. Joan hugged him with the passion of a concerned mother. In her mind, Austin was the product of her actions. She figured that if she hadn't pushed Andrew away, as she did in the early days of their relationship, he wouldn't have turned to Miriam for love, and Austin never would have been born. Joan said to Austin, in a mild tone, "I'm glad that your father isn't here to see you come in like this. You know how he feels about you partying so much." Joan didn't wait for Austin's response to her mention of the tension between him and Andrew about his lifestyle. When she kissed him on the cheek, the smell of alcohol on his breath caused her to cut short their hug. She left him and Walter while she went to shower.

Joan's mentioning of Austin's relationship with his father caused her to ponder on what was going to happen when Andrew confronted Austin about dropping out of school. Something Austin thought was his secret.

Joan was convinced she had done the right thing when she hired a private detective to locate Austin's mother, Miriam. It was as Walter had said, "Everybody should be aware when a loved one was having problems that threatened their life," and that even included Austin's mother who had been gone for seventeen years. As Joan showered, her thoughts carried her back in time. She remembered when she learned that Miriam had cheated on her. Joan was amazed herself how she took things in stride. She remembered thinking, *Hell, I've been cheated on before so the feeling isn't new nor is it something that's unbearable.* To paraphrase an old saying, if it doesn't kill me, it will make me stronger was appropriate.

Joan had become a new person back then able to deal with life's complexities without falling apart. The truth was that Andrew took the news that Miriam and Audrey had a relationship a lot harder than she did. When Andrew learned that the woman he was married to was first lover with the woman that had taken his first wife, it was a lot to bear. It could have been enough to make some men give up on women altogether, but Andrew liked women too much to do that.

Joan's thoughts returned to the present when she heard the faint sound of a voice barely audible over the sound of the shower. She could see the silhouette through the shower door, and when she turned off the water, she heard clearly, "Mom, I'm home."

When Joan exited the shower wrapped in a big, fluffy towel, Crystal hugged her mother ignoring the fact that she was not completely dry. Joan said, with a mother's concern, "You're going to get wet, baby."

The Gathering

Crystal replied, "I know," as she continued hugging her mother.

"Did your brothers come with you?"

"Christian did, he's in the kitchen. A.J. had a paper to finish, but he'll be coming later."

Crystal then started to pick out her mother's wardrobe. She loved coordinating Joan's outfits, but especially her jewelry. Crystal suddenly exclaimed, "Oh this is beautiful, Mom!" She was referring to a bracelet that she hadn't seen before. "Is it new?"

"Yes, your father gave it to me last week."

"Dad always did have good taste. I want to wear this sometime."

Crystal's statement caused Joan to remember that they had to check Crystal's pockets when she was a toddler after they learned that she would transport jewelry from one parent's house to the other. When Crystal got older, she dubbed herself as the little "pack rat." Joan couldn't resist making a joke. She said, while flashing a big smile, "Mommy's little pack rat can wear it anytime."

Crystal, in a drawn out manner said, "Thanks-s-s-s-s Mom." Then both women erupted into laughter. The sound of the phone interrupted them. It was A.J. He was still at school, but was about to leave for the airport. He told his mother that he, Ann, and Eugene would be home in time for dinner.

It was three in the afternoon when Angela and Andrew finished their round of golf. When they got home, the first person they saw was Christian seated on the comfortable sofa. With outstretched arms, Angela was moving toward her nephew, who was now on his feet moving toward her as well. When Christian reached Angela, they hugged. Angela greeted him as her favorite nephew, the same way she referred to A.J., Austin and Eugene when she greeted them. There would always be laughter when the whole family got together and one of the young men would ask their aunt, "Who's your favorite nephew now?" Angela's reply would get just as much laughter when she would say that it's not the one asking me the question. Angela and Walter would have been good parents, but Angela was unable to have children.

Just as Angela and Christian were ending their greeting, Crystal, Austin and Charlene came in from the kitchen followed by Walter, who was coming out of the bedroom finally dressed. A.J., Ann and Eugene arrived minutes later just in time to hug and kiss their aunt and uncle, as their limousine for the airport was pulling into the drive way.

After all the hugging and kissing, Andrew marveled that his six children were together for the first time in a long time. The one outsider, Charlene, would soon join the ranks as family since she was carrying who will be Andrew's second grandchild.

That evening, the women prepared dinner while the men sat around talking and playing games. A.J. and Austin were isolated in a corner talking and playing chess. A.J. asked, "How's she doing?"

"I don't know? All I know is that she is so damn sad. I can't get her to do anything."

"Is she still going to have the abortion?"

"I don't know A.J.…"

The Gathering

The brothers' conversation ended when Joan entered the room and announced that dinner was ready.

It was a good weekend and today had been a fitting end. Andrew and Joan had spent time with their children, but it was now nearly midnight and they were tired. They had to be at the airport at nine tomorrow morning, so they said goodnight to the children telling Ann and Eugene not to stay up too late. They, too, had to get up early.

Young people seemingly always full of energy decided to go for a midnight swim. There was a pool on the premises. Charlene wasn't up for a swim but she encouraged the others to go without her. Eugene decided not to go either, since he had come down with a cold during his school trip.

As the five siblings were leaving for the pool, Eugene said, "Have fun," and then with authority he said, "Boys take care of the girls." He had never said that before, a statement that they heard a lot from their father when they were growing up. Andrew made it clear to his children that the males always looked out for the females. He hadn't said it lately. It probably had something to do with the women's lib movement.

Crystal said, "Thanks, baby brother, but we girls can take care of ourselves."

After the five siblings had left for their swim, Charlene said to Eugene, "I'm going to sit out on the patio until they return. You should go to bed so that you can get over your cold." Eugene agreed and bid Charlene goodnight. Before Eugene could get to his room, he had an overwhelming urge to tell Charlene that he was sorry for her predicament. He had overheard Austin and his father talking earlier in the day.

Luther C. Grayer

When Eugene returned to the patio, Charlene was about to light up. It was a pipe. Charlene sensing Eugene's presence took the pipe from her mouth concealing it as much as possible in her small hand.

Eugene said, "I'm glad that I'm going to be an uncle."

Charlene said, "I'm sure you'll be an uncle a number of times in your life, but not by me. I am not having this baby."

Eugene then walked to Charlene and said, "Give me the pipe."

"No. I haven't done drugs since knowing that I was pregnant, but I need this now. I'm not hurting anybody, since what's in me will never be born."

Eugene said again, "Give me the pipe." He was adamant and when he grabbed Charlene's arm she could feel his strength and knew she couldn't win.

Looking in his eyes, Charlene opened her hand and thrust the pipe toward Eugene. She said, "Take it, you little boy!"

Eugene didn't respond to the "little boy" comment. Yes, he was only seventeen, but he knew he was no little boy. "Where's the rest of the stuff?"

"What rest? I don't have anymore."

Eugene still had Charlene in his grasp. He applied more pressure not saying a word.

Charlene said, "Stop; you're hurting me."

Eugene loosened his grip a little, but he was not willing to let go. "Am I hurting you more than you're going to hurt this baby?"

Reluctantly, with her free hand, Charlene reached in her bra and pulled out her stash.

The Gathering

"This is all I have."

After Eugene disposed of the junk, he and Charlene sat talking. "Don't let them make you have an abortion."

Puzzled, Charlene looked at Eugene. "Who's making me have an abortion?"

Eugene answered with a smirk on his face. "A.J. and Austin; them sleeping with the same woman finally caused a problem."

Charlene, now with an even greater puzzled look, asked, "You mean I'm not the first woman that they both slept with?"

"No. you're not."

Charlene, with anger in voice, asked, "What do they do? Pass women around. When one brother dumps her, the other brother moves in to help her through her bad time and at the first opportunity he's in her panties."

Charlene sat thinking in silence. She was angry with the pair of Casanovas, who passed her around like boys passing around a toy. If her contraceptive hadn't failed her, she wouldn't know now that she had been toyed with.

Suddenly the silence was interrupted when the siblings returned from their swim. As the three brothers approached the patio, Charlene got up and started toward them. She got to A.J. first; she slapped him hard across the face.

A.J. responded with surprise and asked, "What was that for?"

"You treated me like an object throwing me away so that your brother could have his turn." Charlene then walked past Christian to get to Austin. Austin made no attempt to escape. Charlene slapped him too, but this time tears poured from her eyes. She said, "That's for saying that you loved me." Charlene slapped Austin again, and then she turned and left for the bedroom. Crystal and Ann, witnessing the incident from the kitchen doorway, followed Charlene into the bedroom.

The four brothers were now alone, as they would be when they were kids growing up and shared one large room. They would sometimes workout their problems at night in the solitude of their room. Tonight Christian took on his two brothers for what they had done. Christian and A.J. has had an ongoing battle for a while concerning the way A.J. treats Marilyn and now he was involved, in misusing another woman.

While the brothers vented, Crystal, now in the solitude of her bedroom, tried to console Charlene. Crystal knew the game her brothers played, and she let them know that they were jerks. She warned them that one day it was going to catch up to them, and now it had. Crystal and Charlene talked a long time that night. It was good that Ann could fall asleep despite the conversation since she had to leave for the airport so early. Charlene finally managed to fall asleep too and didn't awake that morning when Crystal got Ann up for her trip home.

Crystal stayed up while Andrew and the others prepared to leave. She gave them all big hugs but especially Eugene. Crystal followed Eugene to the kitchen as he went for a bowl of cereal. She asked, "Did Christian tell you what happened at the pool last night?"

"Yes he did."

It was then that Crystal had a flashback of what happened last night.

The Gathering

She had gone back for one last dip in the pool while the others had started for the condo. Her leg got trapped in a piece of netting at the deep end of and she wasn't able to free herself. Christian dove into the pool and freed his sister from what would have been her watery tomb. Christian said, "I only came back because I was reminded of Dad's saying that boys take care of the girls.

Crystal's thoughts returned to the moment and she hugged her baby brother again and said, "I would have drowned if Christian hadn't looked out for me the way you told him to."

At 10:00 AM, Joan, Andrew and the two youngest of their brood were on a plane bound for Chicago. The other four siblings and Charlene were still at the condo having breakfast. Nobody had classes until early afternoon.

Nobody was paying attention to the news being broadcast on television until Charlene noticed that the newscaster was reporting from a location that was familiar to her. She was just there yesterday. It's where she bought her drugs.

Charlene now listened intently and learned that the drugs she had bought were improperly cut and were deadly. More than a dozen deaths had been caused by the bad drugs. Charlene sat silently thinking *me and this baby would be dead if Eugene hadn't taken my stash.*

A.J., Charlene, and Austin were left alone at the condo when Crystal and Christian left for school. The two brothers continued their efforts to convince Charlene not to have an abortion. They apologized for being so callus and not considering the consequence of their actions.

A.J. said, "Have the baby. We'll do the right thing, and then he left for school. He had a 12:00 o'clock class.

Austin and Charlene were left alone at the condo. That's when Austin proposed to Charlene.

Chapter Eleven

Another Workweek

The holiday weekend was over and a new workweek had begun. It loomed to be a very busy week even with Dr. Casey, the third member of the practice, back from a dental conference. Andrew unlocked the door to the office and Joan went to check the alarm system. They were early. Their first appointment wasn't for another hour and none of the help was expected for at least thirty minutes. As Joan perused the mail, Andrew continued on to their private offices.

Dr. Casey was early too. She was sitting at her desk when Andrew entered the office. The two greeted each other with a hug and kisses on the cheeks, which prompted Casey to say, "We can do better than that." She then locked lips with Andrew, thrusting her tongue into his mouth. Joan, who had now made her way to the private offices, stood in the doorway watching. Her thoughts carried her back in time. She recalled her first encounter with Casey at a dental conference.

The two ladies were in the washroom when Joan had to offer assistance by providing Casey with toilet paper. Casey's stall didn't have paper and she couldn't get to any.

After joining Joan at the makeup mirror, Casey said, while showing embarrassment, "I hate when that happens?"

To lighten the mood Joan replied, "I'm tempted to carry my own. Designers can then make sheik purses with pouches for the roll, as if we don't have enough stuff to put in our purses already."

After returning to her table, Joan pointed Casey out to Andrew and asked if he would like to sleep with her. Andrew was shocked. He didn't know if this was a trick question, but he did know that they had promised not to sleep with anyone except each other.

Andrew asked, "Is this a game?"

"No. I'm attracted to her. I thought you might be too."

Andrew couldn't believe what he was hearing. Even though they had lived as a threesome before, it was something that happened and not something that they started out doing.

Andrew, still not sure if Joan was serious or testing him, made a joke. "No, I wouldn't want to sleep with her. She's too skinny for me."

That was anything but the truth and Joan knew it. Casey was beautiful and had a perfect size.

"Too bad; I bet we could get her," said Joan.

Andrew replied "I bet we couldn't."

Joan's thoughts returned to the present when Andrew noticed her standing in the doorway and invited her to join them. When Joan them she received a big kiss from Casey, who declared, "I sure have missed you guys."

Another Workweek

Casey had been away for five days. Normally, as was the case this time, one member of the team would attend a conference while the other two would maintain the practice. On rare occasions, the two women would attend a conference together while Andrew was left to handle the practice.

When Joan and Casey would travel to a conference together, the male dentists, who always out numbered the women, would automatically assume that the two beauties were sisters. It was probably wishful thinking on the part of the men envisioning a romantic interlude. I am sure that the male dentists would imagine themselves enjoying both these beauties together.

The ladies wouldn't correct the assumption that they were sisters, for in truth, Joan and Casey were as close as sisters could be, but Casey now had news that might change that. She didn't waste anytime telling them that she was pregnant. That sounded familiar to Andrew; he had heard it from four different women before. At that moment, he felt awkward, since Casey didn't say whose baby it was.

It was as if Dr. Casey was reading Andrew's mind when she said, "You're going to be a father again, Dr. Grant." Then she made a huddle with her two colleagues and said, "You guys do know that if you don't want to be involved with this, I can take care of things on my own, but I wanted a baby, and at forty, my time is running out."

The day continued to be anything but typical in the challenges that it presented. Andrew had to leave the office to see about his daughter. Ann had passed out in her gym class. She was taken to Northwestern Hospital. Eugene rode in the ambulance with his sister.

On their way to the hospital, Ann's spirit was high. She jokingly said to Eugene, "Your cold is more serious than whatever is wrong with me."

When Andrew arrived at the hospital, it caused memories. It's the hospital where five of his children were born. Andrew inquired about his daughter. He was told that she had been taken for X-rays, and Eugene was in the waiting area.

When Eugene saw Andrew, he said, "Dad, she just passed out in gym class, but they said she regained consciousness a few minutes later. Did they tell you what's wrong?"

"No, not yet, son; they don't know what's wrong yet."

It wasn't long before the doctor who was treating Ann entered the waiting area. He greeted Andrew as mister not realizing that he was a doctor too.

"Mr. Grant, my name is Dr. Mallory. Your daughter's X-rays don't show any abnormalities that would explain why she passed out. We want to keep her here overnight for observation and tests."

With concern in his voice, Andrew asked, "What tests?"

"We want to take blood tests to be sure that her systems are functioning properly before we conclude that her fainting was just due to over exertion which sometimes happen to young women at this stage of development."

Before Andrew could respond to the doctor, Eugene asked, "When can we see her, doc?"

The doctor hesitated for a moment then said, "I need to speak to Mr. Grant alone." After Eugene left, the doctor told Andrew that they would like his permission to conduct a pregnancy test on Ann. The doctor then asked, "Is Eugene her boyfriend?"

Another Workweek

The doctor's request caused Andrew to recall that Joan was the same age as Ann when he got her pregnant. Andrew answered the doctor's question. He told him that Eugene was Ann's brother. He then told the doctor that he would need to talk to his daughter before he could give permission for a pregnancy test. The doctor told Andrew that if they got his permission, it would only be a matter of the lab allocating a small amount of the blood to be used for the test.

As Andrew and Eugene approached Ann's room, Andrew said to his son, "I need to see her alone for a minute."

Eugene said, "You need to ask her if she's pregnant."

Andrew was surprised by his son's statement. "Yes, that's what I need to ask her."

"She's not pregnant, Dad, unless it's by Immaculate Conception. She has never had sex. She would have told me if she had."

Andrew had forgotten how close a brother and sister could be if they were also good friends. It was that way with him and Angela when they were growing up. They shared secrets that they didn't share with anybody else.

When Andrew knocked at his daughter's door, she said, "Come in." She was expecting it to be Eugene since he had come to the hospital with her. "Oh, Dad, it's you. I didn't know you were here yet."

Andrew asked in a serious, but lighthearted manner, "What's this passing out all about?"

"I don't know Dad. It just happened so fast."

Andrew didn't waste anymore time. He told his daughter that they wanted to conduct a pregnancy test. Then he asked her, "Could you be pregnant?"

Ann's response brought joy to this father's heart "Not unless it's from something I ate. Speaking of eating, I'm hungry, Dad." Ann continued in a playful manner, "You do have to have sex to get pregnant, don't you, Dad?"

Before he could catch himself, Andrew murmured, "Eugene was right."

Ann hearing the comment that wasn't meant for her to hear asked, "What did Eugene say?"

"The same thing you just did. He said that you haven't had sex."

"How does he know? Does he think I tell him everything?"

At that moment, their conversation was interrupted by a knock at the door. Eugene figured that his father had enough time to ask his question and get an answer. Ann was sure it was her brother this time. "Entrez frere," she said, which was her version of French meaning, "Come in, brother." They sometimes practiced their French with each other.

Andrew and Eugene stayed at the hospital until visiting hours were over. Eugene took a number of phone breaks. Once, when he went outside for a private conversation with a female friend, Ann's complaining of hunger stopped long enough for her to fall asleep. As Andrew watched his daughter sleep, his thoughts transported him back in time.

Andrew recalled another time that Ann was hungry. It was when Ann was a nursing baby and had to get her mother's stored milk from a bottle when Audrey was away.

One day during Audrey's trial, she'd gotten home later than usual. When she entered the house, Andrew was holding

Another Workweek

his daughter attempting to stop her from crying. He yelled to Audrey, "When you are going to be late, make sure you leave this baby enough milk!"

"I thought I did. Give her to me so that I can feed her." Audrey took her daughter and cradled her in her arms and before she could fully expose her breast, baby Ann had stopped crying. It was as if she knew that food was near and she seemed willing to listen as her mother apologized for having made her wait.

When Audrey did present baby Ann with her favorite feeding apparatus, she latched on and begin to extract the nectar that only a mother could provide. Audrey said, with a mother's flair, "Mommy is so sorry she didn't leave you enough milk." She continued her apology as if baby Ann understood her every word.

Baby Ann continued to nurse only occasionally offering a sigh and then a grunt indicating her forgiveness this time. Then, as if to make it clear that this was not to happen again, her tiny hands, as much as possible, latched on to her mother's breast indicating possession. Audrey responded as if she understood her baby's message. She said again, "Okay, Mommy will never do it again." Baby Ann continued to nurse contently while staring into her mother's eyes.

Andrew's thoughts returned to the present when an attendant entered the room with his daughter's food tray.

Joan came to the hospital as soon as she had finished with her last patient. They left the hospital that night promising that one of them would return early the next day.

The hospital was a busy place early in the morning. With this one being a teaching institution, there were hundreds of bright young future doctors being supervised by the best doctors of various specialties. Her nametag read Dr. M. Chandler, PhD. She was considered one of the best in her field. Dr. Chandler was a Psychologist who taught at the university and supervised upper-classmen in clinical psychology at the hospital. She had only been at the university for a short time having lived in California for the last fifteen years.

This morning, Dr. Chandler was meeting with a group of upper-classmen to visit patients suffering from varying degrees of depression. Dr. Chandler was early so she paid a colleague in neurology a visit. Her friend was supervising a group of future doctors and the first patient they were to see was Ann Grant. Dr. Chandler and her friend talked only for a minute, but they made plans to meet later for lunch.

Dr. Chandler had heard the student doctors mention that Ann Grant was a teenager. Dr. Chandler wondered if it could be the Ann Grant that she knew.

As Dr. Chandler waited for her group, the Grant name caused her thoughts to carry her back in time. It was more than seventeen years ago that she, Dr. Miriam Chandler, PhD. was on trial for murder. She was acquitted after three boys identified her as the woman they saw the day of the killing. Their testimony corroborated Miriam's statement that she was twenty miles away at the time that Morris Minor was killed. The boys had lied during her first trial because they were afraid that they would be in trouble for taking the parking ticket off of Miriam's car.

Dr. Chandler's thoughts returned to the present when one of her students called her name.

Another Workweek

The test conducted on Ann revealed that her bone marrow was deficient in a substance necessary to produce healthy red blood cells. It was the same disease that killed her sister, Drew, twelve years ago.

The disease is hereditary and is passed from mother to daughter. Doctors didn't know much about the disease back then, but they do now. Ann's condition is treatable with daily medication, or it can be nearly rectifiable by the infusion of bone marrow from a suitable donor.

Rather than commit a young and otherwise healthy person like Ann, who has siblings, to a lifetime of medication, the latter option was normally recommended. It's a procedure that has to be repeated every ten to twelve years and a brother and sister of the same father have always been found to be compatible. With Andrew having six children, Ann had a large pool from which to get a donor for the next few decades. Eugene was the most logical choice as the first donor since he was the most convenient.

When tests were conducted on Eugene a few days later, his bone marrow was found to be incompatible to that of Ann's. The lab had never had a case of a brother and sister not being compatible, so they did the test again, and the result was the same. That meant that Eugene couldn't serve as a donor, but it meant even more than that.

When Gina told Andrew that he had another son sixteen years ago, it did occur to him that Eugene might not be his son, but Gina's condition and her plea caused him to except her word and forego DNA testing that would have shown that he was not Eugene's father.

What a mother won't do to protect her child from what she perceives as danger. That even includes fathers whose character constitutes a threat. Somewhere in nature, the male of some species will kill their off spring if not for the mother, who will fight to her death before allowing that to happen.

Gina must have perceived such danger when she determined that her son would be better off with Andrew as a father, rather than the man who might really be his biological father. In Gina's conscious mind, she didn't allow for the possibility that anybody other than Andrew was Eugene's father. She refused to entertain the thought despite having been raped by her husband at the end of her affair with Andrew.

After learning that he wasn't compatible, Eugene told Andrew to call Austin to come home, and then he just walked away.

Andrew called Austin and asked him to fly home to provide bone marrow for Ann.

Austin had talked to his father the night before, as had the other members of the brood. So they all knew that Ann was to get marrow from Eugene. Austin was surprised that Eugene was incompatible; he was also surprised when his father asked him to come home for the procedure instead of asking A.J. or Christian.

Austin was worried. He wondered if his drug use would affect his ability to be a suitable donor. The one good thing was that he hadn't used anything for a while. He stayed off the stuff because he didn't want to entice Charlene. She had decided to have her baby. Austin had convinced her that he loved her no matter whose baby she was carrying.

Another Workweek

After receiving the phone call from his father, Austin sat looking at the coke that he had just scored and was about to consume now that Charlene was staying with her mother for a few days. Austin's treat would have to wait now.

Austin was tested the next day in Chicago and found to be compatible with his sister. The procedure was successfully performed a day later. Now the brother and sister would spend the next two days in the hospital recuperating.

Ann and Austin were placed next to each other in the recovery room. That made it easy for Andrew to keep an eye on them. He had been at the hospital during the entire procedure. Being there caused memories of the past to freely cascade through Andrew's brain. As he sat astride the curtain that separated Ann and Austin, he watched them sleep. They were still under the influence of the anesthesia. At that moment, things seemed so simple. They were safe not having to deal with issues of losing someone they loved. It was something that Andrew wasn't able to protect them from in the past. They both lost their mother and for a while, they had lost their father too.

Andrew's protective vigil was interrupted when Dr. Miriam Chandler tapped him on the shoulder. Andrew was surprised to see Austin's mother. He asked, "What are you doing here?"

Miriam, while pointing to her name tag said, "I work here."

Andrew reading the nametag said, "You're a doctor here?" Then he said, "There's your son."

"I know. My friend told me he was here in the recovery area. She's the doctor who supervised the surgery."

"I can't believe it's coincidental that you and Austin are here after not seeing each other for-r-r-r-r." Andrew having done a quick calculation asked, "What has it been, sixteen, seventeen years since you left?"

Miriam said, "Yes it has been that long."

Even though it was coincidental that Miriam and Austin were at the same hospital, it was not a coincident that Miriam was back in Chicago. Joan had convinced her to come back.

At that moment, Ann was beginning to awake. She could hear talk but it took her a few seconds before she could focus and recognize her father. He was now standing at her bedside. Ann, in a drowsy manner spoke to her father and then to the doctor standing with him.

Ann asked, "How am I doing doctor?"

Miriam said, "I'm not your doctor, but you look great. How do you feel?"

Ann, still drowsy, said, "I feel okay. I don't hurt. Am I going to hurt later?"

"I don't know, Ann. I'm going to let your doctor talk to you about that." Miriam then whispered to Andrew, "Should I go before Austin wakes up?"

"I don't know. Why are you here anyway, Miriam?"

Miriam didn't answer Andrew's question, instead she said, "I don't want to upset him now. I should go and see him later."

Even though Miriam had spoken softly to prevent Ann from hearing, Ann had heard enough to figure out who Miriam was. Ann said, with tears in her eyes, "You should stay and see your son. I wish I could see my mother."

Miriam, now with a hint of a tear in her eye, asked, "Can I hug you?"

Another Workweek

Before Ann could respond, Austin, who had been awake long enough to learn who Miriam was too, said, "Don't let her hug you. She's not a mother. Mothers don't just leave their children." Then he said, "Slide the curtain back. Let me see what she looks like."

Miriam was not the traditionally good mother, and her knowledge of the human psyche had allowed her to over power motherly instincts to pursue other things. She wasn't ashamed of whom she was or of anything that she had done, but her motherly instincts never truly died. When Joan told Miriam that Austin was heading in the wrong direction she allowed herself to be convinced that she could be of help. Miriam slid the curtain open so that she and her son could see each other.

"Oh look you all. She's still pretty."

Miriam smiled. "And you've grown up to be real handsome."

It was not the kind of response Austin was expecting from the woman who, in his mind, had abandoned him. "Is that the best you can do after abandoning me at four years old?"

Miriam, realizing that they could be heard by others in the recovery room, said to Austin, "Let's talk about it when we get you into a room."

"No you abandoned me and all you can say when you come back is that I'm handsome."

Miriam could have postponed their talk by walking away, but Austin might refuse to talk later, so if he needed a public forum to vent his feelings she was willing to go public. She knew that some of the best results come from group sessions anyway.

165

Luther C. Grayer

Miriam said, "I didn't abandon you. I left you with a loving father and two women that were better mothers than I could ever be. Your father was the man that I chose because I knew he was a good man who would do his best to raise you to be a good man too."

Austin's anger became more obvious when he said, "What kind of bullshit is that for a mother to say?"

Miriam remained calm. She was a trained professional. She asked Austin, "Other than me, what else did you miss when you were growing up?"

Austin was amazed. He had envisioned a weeping, apologetic and guilt-ridden woman, who would try to work her way back into his life whenever she returned. This was not who Miriam was. Austin didn't answer her question, and their public session ended when he declared that he didn't want to talk to her anymore.

Miriam refused to allow the session to end there, she said, "You have a right to be angry at me, but you don't have a right to be angry at anybody else nor do you have a right to mess up your life because you're angry at me." Miriam then left the recovery room and attendants came to transport Ann and Austin to their rooms.

The brother and sister were again put next to each other but in separate rooms.

Andrew went with Ann to her room preferring to allow Austin to be alone with his thoughts. Austin wanted to be alone except for his stash. He had been stupid enough to bring it with him from Arizona, but it was at home hidden in the room that he shared with his brothers as a kid. He'd just have to wait until he got out of the hospital and then he'd get high and not think about his mother.

After Ann was settled in, she asked Andrew, "What's going to happen between Austin and his mother?"

"I don't know, baby, but I've got a feeling that Miriam isn't finished yet."

"Tell me some more about my mother. Did she know Miriam?"

Andrew hesitated for a moment, wondering if their conversation would lead to Ann learning that Miriam and Audrey had been lovers before he met either of them.

When Ann didn't get a response, she asked, "Did they meet after I was born?"

Andrew decided that he was going to allow the conversation to take them wherever it did. He was not going to tell any lies about how things happened. He said, "They knew each other before either you or Austin was born."

"Were they still friends when Mom had me?"

"It's a long story, baby."

"Tell me the story, Dad."

Andrew did what Ann asked him to do. He told her the whole story.

When he finished, Ann said, "Wow! They knew each other well!" That wasn't the only family history that Ann was going to get today. After a few minutes of digesting the information, Ann asked, "Where is Eugene?"

Andrew said, "I don't know, baby."

That wasn't the answer Ann was expecting. Andrew always knew where she and her brother were.

Suddenly, while looking at the big clock on the wall, Ann said, "Oh it's still early. He didn't get out of school yet and he's got a big test today." Ann said, "Don't tell him I told you this. He's trying to get an A in chemistry to raise his grade point average. He wants to go to your old school. He really wants you to be proud of him, Dad." Ann didn't know that Eugene's marrow wasn't compactable to hers. She thought that his having a cold was the reason that they used Austin's marrow instead.

Andrew knew that Eugene wasn't in school. The attendance office had called to report that Eugene had been absent, and that he would need a note from a parent to return to school. Andrew thought to himself, *how close Ann and Eugene had always been.* Maybe it was because they were so close in age. Eugene was only a year older than Ann, but from the beginning, he was her protector. He would even try to protect her from their older brothers and sister when they would take advantage of their size and age in dealing with the babies of the family.

Andrew thoughts carried him back in time. He recalled once when Ann was four and wanted Crystal to play with her at her play table using her new tea set.

That day, Crystal was with two of her friends and didn't have time to play the girly tea party game with her baby sister. Eugene was busy too. He was outside playing ball with his brothers; he had no trouble keeping up with them. When Eugene came in for a drink of water, he saw Ann. The door to the room that she shared with Crystal was open. Ann was sitting at her play table when Eugene, though in a hurry to get back to his brothers, went to check on her.

He asked, "Why are you in here alone?"

Ann said, "Crystal is busy and can't play with me. Everybody is too busy."

Eugene, while taking a seat at Ann's play table said, "I'm not too busy."

Ann's voice took on a happy tone when she asked, "Can we have a tea party?"

Eugene went to close the door but didn't do a good job of it. The door remained slightly ajar and Andrew could still hear them talk.

When Eugene got back to the table, he said, "Don't tell anybody that we had a tea party. Okay?"

Ann didn't have to tell anybody. Austin came looking for his brother and when he found him sipping tea, he got on Eugene's case. "You would rather play this girly game than play ball?"

At that moment, Ann must have aged a couple of years because she realized that she had to do something to save Eugene. She said with emphasis, "Go away, Eugene and stop making fun of my table!"

"Yeah; it is funny looking," Austin teased. "Let's go, Eugene. It's your bat."

Eugene went along with Ann's program. "Yeah; let's go," he said, smiling back at Ann.

Eugene was back five minutes later though. He had told his brothers that he had hurt his leg and couldn't play ball anymore. He and Ann played at her little table for a long time that day.

Andrew's thoughts returned to the present when Eugene entered Ann's hospital room. He didn't speak at first, but he finally mustered up the courage to ask Andrew the question. Eugene's words were like bullets to both their hearts.

"When were you going to tell me the truth, Dad?" Then pausing as if realizing he had made a mistake, Eugene said with sarcasm equal to his anger, "Oh, that's right, you're not my dad, are you? You're just a man who slept with my mother and lied about being my father."

Andrew was quick to respond. "I didn't lie to you son. I believed what your mother told me. The marrow test is not conclusive proof of anything."

Eugene said "I want DNA tests so I can know who my father is."

"I'm your father, no matter what DNA tests say."

Ann lay in her bed listening in shock. She had learned earlier that her mother and Austin's mother had been lovers, and now it seems that the person that she has known as her brother all her life might not be her brother.

Ann said out loud, "What other revelations are coming?"

The next day, Ann and Austin were released from the hospital with some restrictions. Good thing they didn't have any place to go anywhere since they were restricted from flying for the next week.

The restriction was for airplane flights not for the flight that Austin was ready to take. When Austin got home, he went to his special hiding place for his stash, but it wasn't there.

Earlier in the week, while packing to leave the house that he had grown up in, Eugene had an urge to check his and Austin's

Another Workweek

special hiding place. He found Austin's coke and flushed it down the toilet.

DNA tests were later conducted and proved conclusively that Andrew was not Eugene's biological father. Eugene was very angry, but not at his mother for her deception, nor at his biological father, who he didn't even know. Eugene was angry with Andrew; the person he had loved the most. He moved out of the family house, insisting on learning who he was. Andrew had no choice but to let him go and hope that he would find his way back home.

A few days after Eugene had moved out, Andrew sat alone in the break room of their office thinking. His thoughts carried him back in time. He recalled when he too wanted to be free to explore his world. It was when Andrew was eight years old.

At the time, Andrew constantly begged his father to let him go somewhere on his own. One day, Andrew and his father were in the park, Andrew saw two boys that lived in the area. He didn't really know the boys, but they had seen each other around the neighborhood. Andrew and the boys struck up a conversation and played for a while. The two boys, having more freedom than Andrew, decided that they were going somewhere more exciting than where they were at the moment.

That day, Andrew had finally worn his father down with his constant pleas to be trusted to go somewhere on his own. Andrew was allowed to go with the boys.

Andrew and the boys' fun conversation changed when they got out of range of adults. They were in an area unfamiliar to Andrew and when one of the boys asked how much money he had, while patting Andrew's pocket, Andrew knew he had made a mistake. Even though Andrew was his mother's only boy, he had older brothers, so Andrew was no stranger to aggression from others. He surprised the one boy who was patting his pocket when he gave him a strong push to the chest causing him to stumble and fall on his butt. The other boy grabbed Andrew from behind and managed to hold him while the other boy, now back on his feet, gave Andrew a hit to the face. Andrew managed to free himself and his defense was much more than the two boys had expected, so they made a hasty exit.

At the time, Andrew felt lost and almost panic stricken wondering if he was going to find his way home. He blamed his father for allowing him to go and now he was lost. Then out of the corner of his eye, Andrew saw a man who looked like his father. The man was partially hidden by a bush, and when Andrew's attention was diverted for an instant, the man wasn't there anymore. Andrew had only seen him for a second and at the time wondered if it was really his father, since the man didn't call to him to show him the way home. Andrew wandered around and finally saw something familiar. He was nearly home. He knew where he was now. When Andrew got home, his father was there.

Andrew asked his father, "How long have you been here?"

"Not long," his father said. "How was your trip?"

At that moment, Andrew knew that his father knew all about his trip. Andrew had lost sight of his father as he struggled to find his way home, but Andrew knew that his father had never lost sight of him. It was one of those times that a father had to let his son go, so that he could find his way home.

Another Workweek

Andrew's thoughts were interrupted when Dr. Casey joined him in the break room. They shared a light kiss since no one was around. They kept their relationship on the down low, preferring that the staff not know that their employers were a threesome.

Andrew touched Casey's stomach and asked, "Is there any chance that this is not my baby?"

"You're having a hard time aren't you, Andrew? You're a good man, and we women know that; that's the reason we want you to be our babies' daddy." Casey kissed him on the lips and put his hand on her stomach again and said, "There is no chance of this being anybody's baby but yours." She then left the break room to attend to her ten-thirty patient, who was waiting in the exam room.

When Dr. Casey entered the room, her patient was sitting in the multi-positional chair with her legs crossed. She had already been prepped by one of the assistants and was waiting for Casey to do her thing. Casey kissed her on the lips and lightly touched her breast and said, "I'm pregnant and it feels so good! I'm going to be a mother and you made me realize that it wasn't too late." Then Casey affectionately said, "Thank you, baby, or should I say thank you, Dr. Chandler for your expert counsel; how much do I owe you anyway?"

Miriam said, "You owe quite-a-bit. You'll be paying me for a long time."

Dr. Casey's thoughts carried her back to three months ago. That's when she first met Miriam, who had just returned to the Chicago area and had gotten a job at the university. That day, she had come to the office to see Joan and Andrew, but they were away at a conference. When she introduced herself to Casey, it was as if Casey had known her for years; Joan and Andrew had talked about her a lot. They had lunch that day and before the weekend, Casey and Miriam had each other.

The next week, Casey got a lot of Miriam's philosophy including her original contention that good men had to be shared. Until now, Casey had accepted the fact that she had chosen a career over a husband and having a family, but being around Miriam caused her to realize that she didn't need a husband to have a family. Casey had a good man sticking it to her regularly, and all she had to do was let nature take its course. Nature did what nature does when Casey stopped taking the pill. Casey's thoughts returned to the present when Joan entered the room.

Joan asked, "What are you two conniving bitches doing now? You've already used my husband's sperms to make your babies."

Casey said, "Yeah and he knows how to deliver those sperms." Casey's statement caused the three women to burst into laughter.

That's when Andrew entered the room; he asked, "What so funny? Is the joke on me?"

Uncannily, the three lady doctors in unison said, "You're no joke." Then, still as if speaking as one, they affectionately said, "To our Dr. Grant with love," they had made that assessment earlier.

The next day was a Friday, but there would be no trip to the condo this weekend. Ann was still recuperating. A.J., Crystal and Christian had flown home to be with the family. Austin, who

Another Workweek

had remained in Chicago after the procedure for his sister, even convinced Charlene to come for the weekend. That evening, nearly the entire family was together; Marilyn, A.J.'s ex-wife and their son Andy was even there. It was like a party, but that's how it is when young people got together. The one person missing was Eugene.

Andy at four-years old was just a doll. Charlene thought in silence, *I might be carrying his brother or sister, but I hope I'm carrying his cousin.*

It was nearly Andy's bedtime; A.J. asked, "Would you like to spend the night, son?"

Andy replied, "Yes, Dad."

"Okay, let's get you ready for bed then." A.J. and Marilyn put their son to bed. As Marilyn kissed Andy good night, he asked, "Is Dad going to take you home tonight?"

"Yes, but he'll see you for breakfast."

"I'll have breakfast with Grandmamma and Granddad. Dad never gets back for breakfast when he takes you home.

A.J. said, "Well I'll see you for lunch then."

Andy was correct; His father didn't get home until Saturday afternoon. He and Marilyn had spent the night at a hotel as they often did when A.J. was in the city.

Later that day when they were alone, Austin hugged his father as if he wanted to give him comfort and to apologize for any worry that his behavior may had caused. Austin told Andrew of his past drug use and of Charlene and the baby's near encounter with death.

Austin said, "I would still be using drugs if you hadn't called me to come home." He told his father that he had convinced

Charlene to marry him. Austin had fallen in love with a woman who was only supposed to be a game. Charlene had fallen in love with Austin almost as soon as she met him. That's why she had been willing to give herself to her ex-boyfriend's brother. It's funny how things happen; sometimes we find love when we least expect it.

Chapter Twelve
Ann and Eugene

It had been more than two weeks since Eugene left home. He hadn't been to school for fourteen days and was in danger of being dropped. It was Friday and as Ann's last class was ending, she came up with the perfect solution. She had to get pregnant with Eugene's baby and then he would have to marry her. Eugene would then be family again and this time forever. It was a simplistic plan for sure and certainly one that had been around for a long time, but in Ann's mind it was original and it would work.

Eugene was living off of money from his bank account. Joan had set up accounts for each of the children with money from their trust fund. Eugene, being eighteen and having money didn't have any problem getting a nice, furnished apartment at one of the residential hotels in Downtown Chicago. Both Ann and Eugene were familiar with the downtown area. They had been there many times with the family.

When Ann called home to tell her father that she was going to visit Eugene, he tried to talk her out of it, preferring that she give Eugene more time to work things out. If Ann had told Andrew her whole plan, he would have sent the police after her.

Luther C. Grayer

Ann got directions to the hotel from the hotel clerk. She was only two blocks away when she got off the train. It was a beautiful day for a walk, and Downtown Chicago was such a pretty place. When Ann got to the hotel, Eugene wasn't there. The clerk, after seeing Ann's I.D., let her into Eugene's apartment instead of making her wait in the lobby.

After being in the apartment for a few minutes, there was a knock at the door. Ann thought it was Eugene, who was knocking because the clerk had told him that she was in the apartment. It wasn't Eugene though. It was one of his neighbors. She was beautiful and ten years older than Eugene. Before Ann could introduce herself, the woman turned and left. The sight of this beautiful woman caused Ann to doubt her ability to pull off her plan. It was like David against Goliath and this wasn't the only beautiful female Eugene knew.

When Eugene finally arrived home, Ann was asleep on the sofa. He expressed surprise and asked Ann, "What are you doing here?"

While yawning Ann said, "I came to see you, since you seemed to have forgotten about your family."

"I don't have a family."

"Don't be silly, Eugene. Of course, you have a family. People don't live together all their lives and suddenly they're no longer family."

At that moment, Ann paused and contemplated what she was intended to do. She thought to herself, *how can I say to Eugene, you are still family and at the same time make plans to have his baby?* Ann was confused, but she wanted Eugene to remain in her life.

Ann and Eugene

Eugene continued to insist that Andrew had lied to him, and that he was not family. Eugene was about to say Dad but caught himself before the word got out. He said, "Your dad lied to me."

"He didn't lie to you. He told you how that happened." After another pause, she said to Eugene, "Suppose I had a baby and I told you that Samuel Adams, a lady's man in their biology class, was the father. You would believe me wouldn't you?"

Eugene surprised Ann when he said, "Hell no! You would never get involved with a loser like that."

Ann had struck a nerve. She didn't know whether that was good or bad. However, what she did know was that she was hungry. "Eugene I'm hungry and you don't have anything here to eat."

"Okay, we'll get something to eat, and then you're going home."

"I'm not going home." Ann was about to say Dad but changed at the last second and said with emphasis, "My *dad* said it was okay that I spend the weekend." She was lying of course, but Eugene didn't know that.

Eugene took Ann to a nice restaurant across the street from the hotel. When they entered, she could tell that Eugene had become a regular there and was a favorite with the female waitresses.

The woman that waited on them was the same woman who had come to the apartment earlier that day. As it turned out, she didn't live in the hotel. She was just paying Eugene a visit before starting her shift at the restaurant. Ann could tell that the woman was angry. Ann figured that she thought that it was one thing to have another woman in his apartment but it was something else to bring her to the place where she worked. For an instant, Ann felt excited to be thought of as the other woman. When Eugene introduced Ann and Mia, Ann could see the anger disappear from Mia's face. Mia responded to Eugene's introduction with a big smile.

"You have a pretty sister."

After Mia had left the table with their order, Ann said, "Now I'm your sister again. Make up your mind, Eugene," and then she said, "Your girlfriend's very pretty, but isn't she too old for you?"

"No she is not. I can handle it."

It wasn't long before they were talking like brother and sister again sharing secrets.

"Yeah, you've been handling things for a long time. I remember my girlfriend Brenda. She told me that you two did it. Why didn't you tell me? You told me about the others."

"I thought you would be angry. It seemed that you didn't want us to get together."

"I didn't and I still don't know why. She was my best girlfriend and you were my best male friend. I felt as if I was going to lose somebody."

The mentioning of Brenda's name caused Eugene to remember his first time. It was with Brenda, and it was her first time, too. Eugene was no more than twelve and was as green as could be about doing it. He still laughed at that first time since he never entered Brenda and neither one of them knew it. Eugene had humped and humped while Brenda laid there with her knees

Ann and Eugene

closed tight enough to hold a dime. After humping and grinding for what was a long time to Brenda, she asked if he was finished. He remembered being proud that he had beaten his buddy in their race to do it first.

Eugene's thoughts returned to the moment when Ann said, "I think it's time for me to try it."

Eugene nearly choked as he was taking a sip of water. "Try what? You don't just try sex."

Ann didn't respond, but she did think in silence, *maybe Eugene's right; maybe you should love the person first and then have sex.* Then she thought, *in that case, my plan might not be so silly after all.*

When Eugene didn't get a response to his statement, he supplied his own. "Just because I do it doesn't mean that you should do it, too."

Ann still didn't respond aloud but continued to think in silence and then suddenly as if tired of trying to figure things out, she said, "I need some more clothes for tomorrow, Eugene."

Eugene asked, "Do you want me to take you home?"

"Not unless we're going home to stay."

Eugene was quick to respond. "I'm never going back there to stay. I'm going to see my father tomorrow."

Ann was just as quick with her reply this time. "Then you need to buy me some new clothes today."

Later that evening they shopped on Michigan Avenue. Ann selected three outfits, which would have cost more than Eugene was prepared to spend. His account would automatically be replenished at the end of the month but that was a week away

181

and Eugene had other expenses before then. He convinced Ann to get only two outfits.

"It's not like you're going to be here that long anyway." Eugene was actually glad that Ann would be with him tomorrow when he would meet his father for the first time.

"You're right." She thought, *this shouldn't take any longer than the weekend. I've got to go back to school Monday.*

After shopping, they walked. Eugene could tell that Ann was tired. He hailed a cab so that they could get back to the hotel where she could rest. As they rode in the cab, Ann was in deep thought, *if I'm going to get pregnant, I should start getting Eugene in the mood.*

Despite being a senior in high school, and obviously a very smart girl, Ann had very little knowledge of sex. She had taken sex education classes, so she knew how babies were made, but she had never come close to being in the position to make a baby.

During the cab ride, Ann rested her head on Eugene's shoulder, figuring this would be a start to getting him ready. Her sex education book said that the male was aroused when the female assumed certain positions relative to him, and this was said to be an arousing position. Ann recalled many times that she had fallen asleep in the back seat of the family car and woke up with her head on Eugene's shoulder. She didn't feel back then the way she felt now. Ann figured that Eugene was feeling something different too. He moved as far to the other side of the cab as he could. Ann thought, *I guess I did it wrong or that this position doesn't work on Eugene.*

Ann and Eugene

When they got to the hotel, Mia was waiting in the lobby. When Mia saw them, she said, "Your sister is still here!" After thinking about how it sounded, Mia apologized to Ann. "You know how it is when you're looking forward to it."

Ann really didn't, but she said, "Yeah I know."

Eugene and Mia continued to talk as Ann started walking away. No sooner than Ann had gotten a few feet from them, a mountain of a man rushed through the swinging doors of the hotel lobby.

He shouted to Mia, "I caught you this time; you and your skinny baby boy. I'm going to break into pieces."

As the huge man moved toward Eugene and Mia, who were trapped by a wall at their backs and furniture to their right and left, Ann knew that she had to save them.

She stopped the man in his tracks when she shouted in the most unladylike manner, "Don't you touch my husband, you son-of-a-bitch." Ann had now positioned herself between the man and Eugene.

She then asked, while looking in the man's eyes, "Mia, who is this man?"

"He's my husband. I'm sorry about this, Ms. Grant; you, too, Mr. Grant." Then Mia took her husband by the hand and said, "Let's get out of here before these people have you arrested."

When Ann and Eugene got to the apartment door, both their hearts were still pounding. Ann took Eugene's right hand and pressed it against her chest so that he could feel her heart beat.

She put her other hand on his chest and said, "Yours is beating fast too." Ann remembered when they were kids. They played games and felt each other's hearts a lot. But it never felt like this before. Now it was as though she was melting. She could never recall feeling so warm. Ann thought, *it's probably because of my surgery or maybe from what happened downstairs.*

Eugene's retreat to the bathroom as soon as they entered the apartment caused Ann to wonder if the downstairs experience wasn't causing him to feel the heat too. She could hear him washing his face for a long time. She thought, *that's one way to cool off.*

Ann called her father while Eugene was in the bathroom. She told Andrew that everything was fine and that she was spending the night at Eugene's place.

Ann was tired but she still had work to do. When Eugene came out of the bathroom, Ann said, "I'm going to take a shower."

"Okay, you take the bed tonight," Eugene said. "I'll sleep on the couch."

It was an efficiency apartment with everything housed in one room. Various areas were separated by either furniture or counters.

When Ann came out of the bathroom, Eugene was asleep. Ann had it all planned. She would come out wrapped in a towel and would accidentally let it slip giving Eugene a full view. That should get him in the mood she thought, but he spoiled it by falling asleep. Then, as if on cue, the phone rang. Eugene jumped up knocking the phone to the floor in the process. Ann, who truly was startled, dropped her towel. Eugene stood there looking at the girl who had grown up as his sister. She was beautiful and she wasn't a girl anymore.

Ann and Eugene

Eugene turned away and said, "I'm sorry I scared you." He then retrieved the phone from the floor. Mia was still on the line. She wanted to know if she could come by tomorrow.

"You told me you weren't married. You could've gotten us hurt if my sister hadn't been there." Eugene ended the call saying, "We shouldn't see each other again."

After Eugene had hung up the phone, he said again, to Ann, who had now rewrapped herself in her towel, "I'm sorry I scared you."

"That's okay. I'm sorry I dropped my towel. Do you have extra pajamas?"

Eugene located a pair of pajamas and gave them to Ann. Ann managed to expose herself again by starting to change before Eugene had completely turned away. Ann thought to herself, *he saw me naked again. I hope that will do the trick.*

Ann knew that it hadn't done the trick when Eugene said, "Goodnight." He was asleep before she could turn off the light.

By morning, Ann had given more thought to her plan and had decided that it was stupid. She and Eugene had loved each other all their lives, but it had been as brother and sister. It was crazy to think that that kind of love could magically change to the kind that a man and a woman have for each other.

Ann sat up in the bed to see if Eugene was still asleep. The couch was empty. She went to the bathroom door and knocked, but there was no answer. She was sad, thinking that Eugene had left without her. He didn't want her there anyway.

Eugene entered the apartment just seconds later carrying two brown paper bags that contained breakfast. "You're awake. Did you get enough sleep?"

"Yes I did."

"Good! I brought us some breakfast, but you need to eat fast so that you can get ready. We need to leave soon."

"What time are we leaving and where are we going?"

"We should leave here in an hour. The bus to the airport leaves in an hour and a half."

With a puzzled look, Ann asked, "Why are we going to the airport?"

"We're flying to Boston and then we're driving to Statesville Prison. That's where my father, Leroy McGee, is."

"How did you find him so quickly?"

Ann's question caused Eugene to remember the day that he met Bob Goodman. He owned a detective agency and was out trying to drum up business. He was passing out flyers that claimed that his agency could locate missing persons in a short time and at a low cost. For a hundred dollars down and proof of one's ability to pay once the person was found was too good of a deal for Eugene to pass up. Goodman accepted a hundred dollars and Eugene's promise of another two hundred dollars if he could get some information about his father in twenty-four hours. Eugene figured that one hundred dollars wasn't too much to risk, especially since he didn't have a clue how to start looking for his biological father.

The next day, Mr. Goodman gave Eugene a copy of a marriage certificate for Leroy McGee & Gina Jones. There was something about Mr. Goodman that caused Eugene to trust him. Eugene gave him the two hundred dollars and two days later Mr. Goodman told him where he could find Leroy McGee.

Ann and Eugene

After Eugene had told Ann the story, she said, "You were lucky to meet such a good detective at just the right time."

"Yeah you're right. I was lucky."

Luck had nothing to do with it. Andrew had arranged the meeting, so that Eugene could find his biological father.

Eugene and Ann got to the bus in plenty of time. They didn't have luggage since they were returning later that afternoon. Ann forgot her cell phone but didn't go back for it, since the bus would be leaving in ten minutes.

It was a typical Saturday morning for prisoner Leroy McGee, who was currently serving ten years for manslaughter. He lay on his bunk thinking of the past. He would replay events in his mind just as they had happened years ago. Recalling the past verbatim as if he was a third party was his way of doing his time. Leroy's thoughts carried him back in time. He remembered nineteen years ago when he fertilized the egg that became Eugene.

It was a chilly night that he stood out of sight as Gina unlocked her apartment door. When she entered the apartment, he rushed in too. Gina was startled, but after she recognized Leroy she calmed down. "What are you doing here Leroy?"

He had been in jail for the last six months and was looking for a warm place to spend the night. Not to mention a warm body to snuggle next to. "I just stopped by to see how my wife was doing."

"I'm fine. Leroy, but I'm tired." As Gina looked towards the door giving Leroy a clue that she wanted him to go, he took a seat on the sofa.

"Did you change those curtains?"

187

Gina became irritated. "It's been six months since you left. A lot has changed. I'm really tired and I want you to go so that I can get some sleep."

"Oh baby, it's so cold outside. Let me stay here tonight so that we can talk more."

"No way; you leave now. We can talk some other time." Leroy's continued plea for refuge was upsetting to Gina. "You leave now or I'll call the police."

Before Gina could get to the phone, Leroy had her in his grasp. He held his hand over her mouth and threatened to hurt her bad if she screamed. That didn't stop Gina from fighting back. But, in the end, she was no match for Leroy. He covered her face with a pillow from the sofa. With her kicking and clawing, Gina was almost unconscious from lack of oxygen. When Leroy ripped off her panties and entered her, she pleaded using the little oxygen that he was allowing into her lungs.

In between gulps for air, she pleaded, "Don't do this. Please don't do this." She begged as much as she could but Leroy used his brute strength to take from this woman her most prized possession.

After Leroy finished his manly act of raping his wife, Gina was unconscious. For a minute, he thought she was dead. The first thing that Leroy said, after noticing that Gina was still breathing, was, "I'm sorry. I didn't mean to hurt you."

As Gina made her way to the bathroom, she grabbed her purse and shouted at Leroy. "Why did you do this to me?" After locking the bathroom door, she called the police. They were there in three minutes, but Leroy was gone. He was later arrested

Ann and Eugene

but never went to trial. The D.A. didn't think that he could prove rape against a husband.

During the next nine months, Leroy saw Gina from a distance, but she never saw him. That was until the day he came to the hospital after she had given birth to Eugene.

When Gina saw him, her first words were, "Get the hell out of here, you son-of-a-bitch, and don't you ever come near me or my baby again."

Others on the floor could hear Gina's outburst, including Morris Minor who just happened to be there that day to pick up his sister. Morris and his sister had grown up in Chicago; his sister was now a nurse at the hospital. Leroy bumping into Morris, on his way out of the building, was a coincidence. Leroy was from Chicago, too, and he and Morris knew each other from their high school days.

Eugene was six months old when Gina learned that she had cancer. That was when she told Leroy that she had been blackmailed by a man named Morris Minor and that she had killed him.

Morris had gotten the idea to blackmail Gina after learning, from his sister, that Gina's baby was given the sir name Grant. Leroy had told Morris that Gina and he were married and that the baby was his. Morris, being the opportunist that he was, looked into the matter further and saw a chance to make some money. He threatened Gina, promising to tell the Grants that Eugene was not Andrew's son. Morris was a real pig. He made Gina fly to Boston to perform sexually as well as pay him money to keep his mouth shut.

Luther C. Grayer

After Gina learned that she was dying, she paid Morris her final visit to determine if she could trust him to keep their secret once she was dead. Morris failed the test. He reacted as if he was sad that Gina was dying, while at the same time groping her refusing to relinquish what might be his last chance to have her. Leroy thought to himself if Morris had known at the time that it was the last time that he would see Gina's beautiful jewel or any jewel for that matter, I'm sure he would have cherished the moment more. Imagine what Morris must have thought at the end: the jewel giveth and the jewel taketh away.

Leroy's thoughts returned to the present when his cell door opened; it was time for lunch.

Leroy had raped Gina nineteen years ago, but he was the only one that she could totally confide in. Gina needed him for relief from the guilt of killing a person. Leroy's guilt for what he had done made her secrets safe with him. He took the gun that Gina had used to kill Morris and was seen throwing it in a pond. The gun was later recovered and used as evidence to convict him of the killing.

Leroy gives testament to the true compassion of mother's for each other. Gina told him of her relationship with Miriam and Joan. Gina needed sexual relief and that was fulfilled by her fellow mothers. They wanted to make her dying easier; Leroy image the beauty of Miriam, Joan and Gina as a threesome. The three women continued as lovers until Gina died.

Gina regretted that Miriam had to be tried for killing Morris, but she couldn't tell the truth since it would lead to Andrew learning that he wasn't Eugene's father. Gina was relieved

Ann and Eugene

when Miriam was acquitted. Gina had done what she thought was necessary to protect her son and she trusted Leroy to do the same.

Leroy had been raised by a father who had been a crook all his life. That's what Leroy saw and that's what Leroy became. That's why he was glad that Eugene was being raised by an honest man. Leroy didn't complete high school, but he was smart enough to know that at birth you are not who you are going to be. You become the person you are, based on your upbringing.

The meeting between Eugene and Leroy came and went. Leroy told Eugene the story of his creation and of his mother's effort on his behalf. Eugene left the prison that day more confused than ever.

When Eugene joined Ann in the waiting area, she seem tired from the flight. During their cab ride to the airport Eugene pondered his situation. He questioned whether he was a different person by virtue of knowing from whom he came. He wondered if he could trust his reactions to life or if he had to guard diligently his every response for fear of being Leroy. He didn't like Leroy.

It was five that evening when the plane landed in Chicago. While Eugene and Ann sat waiting in the terminal for the bus that would carry them to the downtown area, Ann laid her head on Eugene's shoulder. This time, there was no romantic purpose to her gesture. She was just sleepy. The sound of Eugene's cell phone, which was in his shirt pocket near Ann's ear, didn't even disturb her sleep.

The call was from Andrew, who had called Ann a number of

times that day and got no answer. "Where are you and where's Ann? I can't get her on her cell."

"She's fine other than being sleepy. She went with me to see..." After some hesitation Eugene continued, "She went with me to see my father."

Eugene's statement caused Andrew instant anger, but he realized that was no good. He quickly got his emotions in check and asked to speak to Ann.

Even though Andrew tried to remain calm, Eugene, having been raised by this man, could hear the concern in his voice. Eugene's concern grew, too, but not because of his and Andrew's situation. Ann wouldn't wake up.

Eugene shouted, "She won't wake up!"

Andrew and Eugene lost communication when, in his excitement, Eugene dropped his cell phone. By this time, people had gathered around to offer assistance. It wasn't long before medical help was on the scene. One Good Samaritan, who had retrieved Eugene's cell phone, gave Andrew information as to which hospital the ambulance was taking Ann.

When Andrew got to the hospital's emergency room, he saw Eugene sitting in the waiting area. He had his head buried in his hands. Andrew touched Eugene on the shoulder and asked if the doctor had said anything about Ann's condition.

Before Eugene could answer Andrew, a doctor approached them. He asked Andrew, "Are you her father?"

"Yes I am. How is she?"

"She's is suffering from Narcoleptic Induced Syndrome due to atmospheric pressure changes during her flight. I need to ask

Life Goes On

you, Mr. Grant, if you and your daughter were advised that she shouldn't fly too soon after her operation?"

"Yes, we were told that she shouldn't fly for a week. It's been more than three weeks now since her surgery."

The doctor said, "We might need to require a longer period of restriction in the future.

"Did I do this to her?" Eugene asked. "She was on that plane because of me."

"You didn't know that she shouldn't fly and she thought it had been enough time since her surgery. If I had known that she was thinking about getting on a plane, I would have stopped her. But that's just what fathers do."

The doctor said to Andrew and Eugene, "Not only must we be concern that she awakes, but that she awakes without brain damage."

Chapter Thirteen

Life Goes On

It had been six weeks since Ann's sleep-induced condition began. Eugene was at her bedside every day. He had heard that a person in a coma could hear and that the sound of loved ones would keep them alive until they could recover. He would sit talking and watching Ann sleep, causing him to remember over and over again their last night in his apartment. His thoughts carry him back in time to that night.

He had pretended to be asleep, but he couldn't get the picture of Ann out of his mind, as she stood naked in the middle of the room. It was just for a moment that he saw her naked, but later that night she was just a few feet away asleep in his bed. Went he stood next to the bed, she looked so peaceful lying there and he was helpless in his quest not to touch her.

Eugene's touch scared Ann, but once she realized it was him, she pushed back the covers and invited him in. They melted into each other as they embraced and then they made love. It was Ann's first time, but that kind of lovemaking was Eugene's first time, too. It couldn't have been better. After their passionate lovemaking, Eugene returned to the sofa. It was as if he had done something wrong and didn't want the light of day to give testament to his misdeed.

Eugene's thoughts were suddenly interrupted when Andrew rushed into the room. He grabbed Eugene by the neck and threatened to kill him for doing this to Ann.

"You did this to her to get back at me!" Andrew shouted.

Eugene offered no resistance; he did feel that it was his fault that Ann lay in a coma. He wanted to be punished. He wanted someone to hurt him. He wished that he could lie down and die for Ann's return.

Andrew, now sobbing, said, "Both her and the baby are going to die because of you."

Eugene was both surprised and horrified. He also sobbed.

"Is she pregnant?"

"Yes she is."

" Is it your baby?"

"It's my baby. But I didn't know that she was pregnant and I didn't do it to hurt you. I love her too much to use her for something like that."

Eugene then leaned over Ann's motionless body and sobbed pitifully for her to awake. He wished that she would awake to his touch as she did that night in his apartment. He wanted to tell her how much he loved her. He had never said those words to her as a man to a woman.

Eugene had felt like a rapist ever since he and Ann made love. He felt that he had taken advantage of her, and when he met his biological father, he was convinced that it was in his genes. Only now was it clear to him that his brotherly love had changed that night. He didn't just love Ann. He was in love with her.

During the next month, Eugene continued his constant vigil at Ann's bedside. The staff ignored visiting hours allowing him to sit and talk for hours to Ann. He talked about things that they had done as children. Their lives became well known on the floor, with the workers getting bits of information every day. Ann's room, 713, was near the elevator, so even Andrew had walked in on talk sessions and learned things that he didn't know.

Andrew had the authority to pull the plug if necessary, but it was obvious to him that he couldn't love Ann any more than Eugene, so he promised that they would make the decision together if they had to let her go.

It was 11:30 PM and Eugene was at his apartment. He was just awakening from what was to have been a ten-minute respite that started at six that evening. When he got to the hospital, Ann's room was empty. He went to check the nurse's station, which was a beehive of activity with people he didn't recognize. Before he could ask about Ann, he heard two nurses as they were getting on the elevator talking about the patient in room 713. Eugene managed to corral the attending doctor, who he didn't know.

Eugene asked the doctor anxiously, "How's the patient that was in room 713?"

The doctor asked Eugene, "Are you the father of the expected baby?"

"Yes. How are they?"

The doctor was reluctant to answer Andrew's question; he

said instead "Her father is on his way here now. Why don't you have a seat until he gets here?"

Eugene, with insistence in his voice, said, "No! Tell me now! How are they?"

The doctor asked for the patient's chart, which the nurse couldn't locate at the moment, but she did say that the father had given permission to give the baby's father all the information.

After a moment's hesitation, the doctor said, "I'm sorry. Both mother and baby are dead. There was nothing we could do. Her father gave permission for us to stop life support."

Eugene was in a daze. He just turned and left. On his way out of the hospital, he passed an elderly man, who was crying as if he, too, had lost someone. When the elderly man reached the attending doctor, he introduced himself as Mr. Taylor.

The doctor was now holding the chart of Mr. Taylor's daughter and her unborn baby. The patient had been allowed to die earlier that day after a third unsuccessful surgery. Her baby was dead before the last surgery was completed. Ms. Taylor was the victim of an automobile accident, and was assigned to room 713, which was vacated earlier that day.

The doctor said to Mr. Taylor, "The baby's father was just here. Did you see him on your way in?"

The grieving father said, "No."

The doctor was so busy that he didn't give it more thought.

As Eugene crossed the street after leaving the hospital, he was almost hit by a car. He thought to himself, *that would have been perfect.* At that moment, he wanted to die more than ever. When Eugene reached his car, his cell phone rang. The caller

ID indicated that it was Andrew. Eugene didn't answer. He was angry that Andrew had made the decision to let Ann go. He drove to the beach, which wasn't far from the hospital. Andrew would take him and Ann there when they were kids. They would have such a good time playing in the water. Now Eugene was going for one last swim. His cell phone wouldn't stop ringing, so he threw it in the lake. He didn't need a phone anymore.

As Eugene prepared for his midnight swim, he met a man who had returned from docking his boat. The man spent a few seconds trying to engage Eugene in conversation, but Eugene's focus was elsewhere, so the man left. Eugene stripped down to his shorts. It was a mild night and the water felt good on his feet. As he waded into the lake, the water was calm. It seemed to invite him to trudge forward. It was as if the water promised to relieve his pain.

When Eugene reached the drop-off, the water, though still calm, was now in control. It determined Eugene's direction carrying him more into the dark. Eugene's thoughts were now of the permanency of it all. Death was all consuming and when you're dead, there was no more. Eugene's commitment to die was wavering, and suddenly, he realized he didn't want to die.

Eugene wanted to make it back to shallow water. The view of lights from shore seemed to flicker on and off, as if someone was playing with the switch. It was the choppiness of the Lake bobbing him above and then below the horizon that caused the lights to be intermittently visible. It was difficult for Eugene to maintain a direct path back to shore and he was already tiring. It wasn't long before he realized that he was at the mercy of the

Life Goes On

current and to fight it head on would only render him helpless in his attempt to get back to shore.

Eugene asked for help. It's not clear if he was a Christian even though he had been baptized. Most kids traveled the direction indicated by their parents. Eugene was a church person, since Andrew and Joan had raised him so that he would have a sense of God. Although Eugene had a sense of God, he had never been in such dire straights before, so he never had to call on God with such urgency. The will to life propelled him to new heights.

As Eugene called to God for help, calm came over him causing him to relax and go with the flow. He saw images. At one moment, it was his deceased mother and the next moment it was someone else who he had known before their death. Eugene couldn't determine if the images were there to welcome him to death or to encourage him to continue his quest for life. Eugene chose to believe the latter, since death was guaranteed to us all but why not later, instead of now.

It might be that near death experiences allows one to communicate with those who have passed on. That was Eugene's experience. His mother was there. She offered no apology during her spiritual appearance for what she had done in life. It was as if she wanted him to know that he was entitled to a good life and he should make the most of his chances. It must be that messages can also be sent to others. That's what happened in Eugene's case when Richard's spirit appeared. His message was for his grieving brother, Walter.

Richard's spirit said, "Tell Walter my flesh was weak for Earth's trappings but my belief in God was real. I am in a better place now. Tell him to stop grieving for me."

Luther C. Grayer

As Eugene continued to struggle, it was becoming clear to him that he wasn't going to be able to deliver Richard's message. Then he saw the light! No! Not from heaven! The light was from a boat, and then Eugene heard the faint voice as it called for help. On second thought, maybe it was a light from heaven, since Eugene was about to go under. He had only enough energy to make it to the rowboat. When Eugene climbed aboard, he saw the man that he had seen earlier on the beach. The man was now unconscious and wet, seemingly from perspiration rather than from the lake water. Eugene figured he had had a heart attack. Eugene did what he could to comfort the man while using the man's cell phone to call for help. He then started to row to shore. Eugene managed to get him and the boatman back to shallow water where help was waiting.

Eugene and the man were rushed to the hospital. The boatman was wheeled in on a stretcher while Eugene insisted on walking into the emergency room. He was merely exhausted from his swim.

When the nurse saw Eugene, she yelled to him. "Where have you been?" Then realizing that the volume of her question was inappropriate, she rushed to Eugene's side. "She's showing signs of waking up."

Eugene was instantly aware that the nurse was talking about Ann and that he had gotten something wrong. The nurse told him that she had been moved to intensive care earlier that day after showing signs of recovering. Eugene cried as he said, "Ann's alive, and so am I; thanks to the man in the boat."

It was later learned that the boatman was rowing back to his docked boat when he suffered a heart attack. He would have died if he hadn't received help in time.

Two weeks later, Ann awoke. It happened when Eugene leaned over her and tears fell from his eyes wetted Sleeping Beauty's face. As Eugene wiped away his tears from Ann's face, she startled him. She opened her eyes but didn't speak. She showed no sign of recognizing Eugene. Eugene pushed the button to call the nurse, which went unanswered.

That's when Ann asked while yawning, "Where am I?"

Eugene, who had been talking nonstop for almost two months, was at a loss for words, but he eventually managed to answer Ann's question.

After Ann was awake for a while, she learned that she was pregnant, and she realized what it felt like to carry another living being inside her body. Her motherly instincts were immediate, and she was as happy as she had ever been. She was about to be a part of the process that keeps the population replenished.

Within a week, Ann was involved in an exercise program to strengthen the muscles that had only moved because of outside stimuli for almost two months. She had to move slowly and regain her knowledge of how to do things. It took more than three months for Ann to recover sufficiently to walk down the aisle as Eugene's bride. It was another wedding at Luke's big house.

On their wedding night, Ann didn't know exactly what to expect. They hadn't had sex but that one time. Eugene hadn't touched her since then despite the doctor giving them the all clear. Eugene said he didn't want to hurt the baby.

Luther C. Grayer

That night, an inexperienced Ann tried to entice her husband to partake of her goodies. When she couldn't bring his manhood to attention, she cried. She figured it was her bulging belly that was unattractive to him, or maybe what happen that one time wasn't good to Eugene and he just didn't want her anymore. Whatever was the problem, it made her cry. Ann felt rejected. Then, she realized that she didn't know much, so she said, "Tell me what you want me to do."

Eugene was so engrossed at the fact that his manhood didn't instantly spring to attention that he only now realized that Ann thought it was because of something that she wasn't doing right. His manhood had never done this to him before. It had sprung to attention at just the thought of a woman's jewel and now it lay limp with a beautiful jewel just an inch away waiting to be entered. He didn't understand it.

He said, "It's not you, Ann. I don't know what it is, but I'm sure it's not you."

Later that night they fell asleep in each other's embrace hoping whatever was the problem would be gone by morning. Ann was awakened three hours later by abdominal pains. Eugene, with the help of Andrew, rushed Ann to the hospital where she was treated. Ann was almost six months pregnant. Her due date was easy to calculate, since she had only had sex once. She was suffering from a rare condition called Premature Clampcia, a condition that caused her system to go into birth mode prematurely. Symptoms are often triggered by sexual excitation.

Ann was put on bed rest and restricted from all sexual activity until future evaluation. This condition may have been the cause of the death of Ann's mother during the birth of her second child some fifteen years ago.

The next morning, as Eugene sat watching Ann sleep, he couldn't help but wonder what would have happened if he'd had sex with her last night. It was at that moment that he had an overwhelming urge to see Walter to give him Richard's message. Eugene was reluctant to deliver a message from a deceased person. He wondered if Walter would think that he was crazy. It didn't matter though, something within was in control. He had to deliver Richard's message.

Eugene made a special trip to Walter's house. As he stood at the door waiting for someone to answer the bell, he realized that he had come at the wrong time of day. Walter was still at work and Aunt Angela was out of town. When Eugene turned to leave, the door opened. It was Walter. Walter said that he hadn't felt well earlier, so he didn't go to the office today. Eugene figured Walter had been lying around all the day, since the house was dark, with the curtains still drawn letting no light in. The house felt cold to Eugene.

After Eugene delivered Richard's message, along with the circumstances behind it, Walter didn't question its validity. Instead, he cried. It wasn't a sad cry though. It was the kind of cry that Andrew had at Ann's wedding when he realized that she was no longer his little girl. There are good cries and this was a good cry. Eugene then saw the gun lying on the table. It was almost hidden by a piece of paper.

When Walter saw Eugene looking at the gun, he said, "I

was checking it. There have been a number of burglaries in the neighborhood lately." Then he said, "I lock it up before Angela gets here. Guns make her nervous."

Eugene and Walter hugged. Eugene didn't know if Walter was telling the truth about why he had the gun out, but he did feel that Walter wanted to live. Maybe when you come as close to taking your own life as Eugene had, you develop a second sense about these things.

As they hugged, Eugene knew he had done the right thing. He could feel in his heart that Walter had gotten real comfort from Richard's message.

It was about this time that Eugene concluded he had a calling. I suppose a person's calling to serve God was an individual thing, but you would think that it would involve direct communication with God. This was how Eugene interpreted his experiences. He was convinced that God was talking through him and that he was being called to serve. God had delivered him from near death, saving him for future work and he was excited about it.

During the remainder of Ann's pregnancy, she and Eugene were restricted from any sexual activity. They were even encouraged not to sleep together until after the baby's birth. When it was time for Ann's baby to be born, Eugene was a dutiful father-to-be. He took Ann to the hospital. She had grown large during her last month. Eugene helped her through eight hours of labor. He was great in the delivery room; that is until the episiotomy. When the doctor made the incision to Ann's jewel, Eugene almost passed out, but he got through it. It was only a few minutes later that Ann delivered a son.

A.J.'s Pursuits

That wasn't the only delivery occurring for the Grant family. Three months earlier, Dr. Casey had a boy too while Charlene had a girl. Tests revealed that Andrew was the father of Dr. Casey's baby just as she had said. Miriam and Casey became a couple. Casey stopped working to stay home with her son. She planed to work again some day, but for now she was totally fulfilled being a mother.

Austin and Charlene had married three months before Charlene's baby was born. The whole family was at the wedding. It was a joyous occasion held at Luke's big house as so many weddings had been before. Austin had reconciled things with his mother. He had been angry at Miriam for years for leaving him, but he came to realize how true it was that she had left him in good hands. If it's true, as was stated earlier, that motherly instinct for her child never dies, then it's probably true that a son's love for his mother never dies either. Austin learned that after getting something you wanted, it may not be what you want. Let's hope that it doesn't turn out that way with his marriage. After Charlene's baby was born, tests proved that A.J. was the father.

Chapter Fourteen

A.J.'s Pursuits

It was now September and A.J. was beginning his teaching career. It was his first day on the job. He had graduated from college two months ago and had returned to Chicago to teach at an inner city high school. A.J. was very familiar with the school since Chatham high defeated his school in the state basketball play-offs three years in a row. A.J. was a member of his school's team during those losing years.

Chatham high was recently renamed Jesse Jackson Academy which A.J. couldn't get used to. He still referred to the school as Chatham. A.J. was still getting used to hearing his real name too, since Andrew Grant was on his ID and that's how he was addressed at the school.

It was five years ago that A.J. was in high school and now he was about to teach freshman and supervise a senior division. A.J. was less than four years older than some of the seniors that he would be supervising.

It felt good to earn a living. Even though A.J. was a member of a wealthy family and would inherit a fortune one day, he wanted to work just as his parents did. And he had always wanted to be a teacher.

The end of the workweek was cause for celebration, and A.J. went to a club that was popular at the time. It was there that he met Pauline. She was one of three dancers performing that night. Pauline was beautiful with a body that did complete justice to the skimpy outfit she wore. It commanded attention and got it from A.J. and all the other men in the place. A.J. offered to buy her a drink, which she accepted. They talked during her breaks and A.J. stayed until the last show. He offered her a ride home hoping to get into her pants. Pauline accepted the ride but wasn't giving it up. She did give A.J. a kiss for the ride home and promised to have dinner with him another day.

Pauline and A.J. had dinner. A.J. learned that Pauline didn't drink and what she accepted from patrons at the club was club soda at Perrier prices. After dinner, they went to the Museum of Science and Industry to view the latest attractions. The two went out for another week before Pauline ended up at A.J.'s apartment.

As they sat on the sofa, A.J. followed up on his first kiss. He leaned over and locked lips with Pauline, but this time their tongues made contact. Pauline was wearing a dress and A.J.'s hand had found its way under it. He massaged her jewel. His action caused her panties to become wet. He now used both hands to lower her pantyhose along with the panties allowing the jewel to breathe. He then got down on his knees and removed Pauline's shoes, allowing him to free her of her underwear. The lower half of her body was now exposed.

Luther C. Grayer

A.J. scrutinized the beauty of Pauline's body, but he didn't lose focus. There was still work to be done. He had to free the top half of this magnificent structure of the apparels that encumbered it, and then he would be able to enjoy the loveliness of it all. A.J.'s efforts were rewarded. His manhood was so at attention that it threatened premature launch. He kept things under control though, and when Pauline undressed him they were both ready to make love.

Having now made their way to the bed, A.J. was about to put on his condom.

Pauline asked in a panic, "It's not latex is it? I forgot to tell you, I'm allergic to latex."

"I don't know." In the heat of the moment he didn't think of the obvious, but asked instead, "How can I tell?"

"The label; read the label, baby." He had thrown the condom rapper across the room, so he read the cover of one of the other half-dozen condoms still on the stand next to the bed.

"They're all latex," he said. "Do you have any with you?"

Pauline said, "No I don't. Despite what you might think, I don't do this often, so I don't carry condoms." Then she said, "I'm okay for sex; my period ended yesterday so you don't need to use a condom this time."

Then she had an afterthought, "You don't have any sexually transmitted diseases, do you?" They had sex that night relying on the rhythm method of contraception.

That Monday at work, A.J. was standing outside his division room welcoming his students in. That's when he got a glimpse of a woman who looked like Pauline. She was closing the door to a division room down the hall. With only ten minutes for division, A.J. couldn't leave to get another look at the woman, but maybe, if he was fast enough, after division he could get a second look.

A.J. was out the door as soon as the bell rung, but the other division had already left by the time he made his way to the room. He did learn that the division teacher's name was Ms. Johnson, and that was not Pauline's last name. A.J. figured he had been mistaken and just had Pauline on the brain.

A.J. was one of three teachers who had fifth period lunch duty that day. As he walked around encouraging students to put away their trays, he saw her again. She was dressed impeccably sitting with two male students; one of them was wearing a shirt and tie. When A.J. touched her on her shoulder, she looked up and was surprised to see him. Her two companions picked up their trays while excusing themselves; they said they had to go to the library before leaving school.

Pauline asked, "What are you doing here? Did you follow me?"

A.J. was surprised at the question. "No I didn't follow you."

"Then what are you doing here?" Before he could answer her question, another teacher introduced herself. She was wearing her coat, as if she was about to leave the building.

Ms Conroy reading A.J.'s name tag said, "Hi Mr. Grant." She had seen him in the office before, and then she said, "I see you've met Pauline. She's one of our top students. She'll be graduating the end of this year. Get your coat Pauline; it's time for us to leave." Ms Conroy and two other students were attending a conference this morning for future English teachers.

Luther C. Grayer

It wasn't until that Friday that A.J. saw Pauline again. He had been tempted to check her program to find out where she was during the school day, but he didn't. It was as if seeing her at school as a student would affect how he felt about her on the weekend, and he sure wanted to see her that way again.

That night at the club, when Pauline joined him at his table she greeted him by his full name. "Good evening, Mr. Andrew Grant."

A.J. responded in kind. "Good evening to you, Ms. Pauline Hunter."

They talked while Pauline sipped her high priced club soda. She asked, "Are you going to take her home tonight?"

"Yeah, but I'll come back to get you." He didn't want to see the men look at her dance; he knew what they were thinking.

That night as they drove to his apartment, A.J. couldn't resist touching Pauline's jewel. He held on to it for a moment unwilling to turn it loose.

She warned him, "You should wait until we get to the apartment. You could have an accident like this."

A.J. laughed. "You've heard that song too."

With a puzzled look, she asked, "What song is that?"

He explained that there is an old blues song that tells about a dog walking along a railroad track and a train ran over his tail cutting off a piece. The dog was in such a frenzy looking for his tail that he didn't see the other train coming, and was struck and killed. The song ends harmoniously saying dog killed trying to get a little piece tail.

Pauline said, "Oh, that's what I'm; a piece of tail."

A.J.'s Pursuits

"No, that's not what I meant." Then attempting to change the subject, A.J. asked, "How did you get started dancing in clubs so young? How old are you anyway? You know it's against law if you're less than eighteen."

Pauline hesitated then said, "My mother and I were homeless three years ago. Now we have an apartment and plenty of food to eat." After a pause, she paraphrased the lyrics of a song to make her point; "Use what you got to get what you need."

Pauline told her story. She's nineteen and a year behind in school because she missed most of her freshman year. She had to earn money for her and her mother to live on, since her father had left when she was six, and her mother was always sickly and unable to maintain a full-time job. Things were tough for her growing up.

That night Pauline looked especially good to A.J. He had been looking forward to this ever since the one time they did it. As they sat making out on the sofa, things weren't progressing as they should. A.J.'s manhood wasn't rising to the occasion; it was lying down on the job. Pauline did her part, but there was no erection to be had. A.J. concluded it was mental. He might be feeling guilty that he was doing something immoral by having sex with a student. He told Pauline what he thought. She agreed and said that they would work on it next week. She was going on a school trip to Western Illinois University for the rest of the weekend.

A.J. couldn't wait until next week; he wanted to get back in the saddle to make sure that everything was alright down there. After taking Pauline home, he called Marilyn's cell phone. She was asleep, but he was able to convince her to have a late night drink with him. A.J. didn't wait until they got into his apartment; he gave Marilyn a tongue felt kiss at the door. He could feel his manhood start to swell. By the time they got into the apartment he had Marilyn nearly undressed and when he touched her jewel, he knew he was ready.

They made love in those early morning hours, and as A.J. drifted off to sleep, his last thought was that his problem was mental.

Marilyn laid next to A.J. watching him sleep; she had missed waking up in his bed on weekends when he was in town. This was the first time they had made love for more than two months now. Marilyn figured he had found himself another girlfriend, as he did quite often.

She spoke his name softly, "A.J., wake up. It's time to get up."

A.J. responded with a yawn, but eventually asked, "What time is it?"

"It's 7:00AM and I've got to go."

"Why so early?" A.J. asked while massaging Pauline's breasts.

Pauline said, "Our son, Andy, has a dental appointment. I would like to stay for another round, but I just don't have time."

Marilyn was surprised when A.J. said, "I'll go with you."

After Andy's dental appointment, the three of them went to Navy Pier for a kid's interactive show. That was the first time that Andy met his sister. Austin and Charlene were at the show

A.J.'s Pursuits

with six-month-old Constance. Andy had a great time with Constance. At five years old he didn't know that she was his sister. Being his mother's only child he didn't yet have a concept of siblings. The larger problem would be for the adults. What would they tell this brother and sister one day? At that moment A.J.'s thoughts carried him back in time. He recalled how he and Austin's sharing girls got started.

At the time A.J. was a lady killer, they were attracted to him like bees to honey. Austin on the other hand was shy which limited his female relationships. He and A.J. had always been close. A.J. encouraged Austin to be bolder; he remembered when he didn't have confidence either.

One day when Austin was being bolder with an older girl that he liked, she embarrassed him in the presence of her friends. A.J. witnessed the incident. A few days later, A.J. had won the affection of the girl that had embarrassed his brother and a week after that, he had her eating out of his hand. He made her apologize to Austin, and even though he didn't tell her to sleep with Austin, she did. That was the first time that the brothers had shared a girl, but it wasn't the last. It became a game for them.

A.J.'s thoughts returned to the present when Austin said, "We have to go brother. Constance has a doctor's appointment." The brothers hugged as they said goodbye.

Andy was worn out from the day's activity. He went sound asleep as soon as A.J. put him in his car seat and didn't awake when A.J. carried him into the house. After Marilyn put Andy to bed, she and A.J. went back to A.J.'s place for round two.

That Monday Pauline decided that earlier would be better

than waiting for the weekend to raise Lazarus, so she paid A.J. an unexpected visit. A.J. was surprised when he opened the door and saw her standing there. She gave A.J. a kiss and brushed passed him on her way into the apartment. Pauline directed A.J. to take a seat in the big chair that faced the sofa. She then made her way to the sofa for her show.

Some men would say that there is nothing more arousing than watching a woman undress herself. A.J. was one of those men; he gave Pauline a standing ovation, and he never got out of his seat. They had sex that night and a lot of other nights after that; two months later Pauline learned that she was pregnant.

Monday was the beginning of the fourth marking period at Jesse Jackson Academy and there were two student teachers beginning their internship there. They were being reassigned because the school, where they were originally, no longer had Honors classes, and Marilyn and Mark had to practice teach the more advance classes to meet their graduation requirements.

The two student teachers met with Assistant Principal Warren Bibs, who was on the fast track to becoming Principal of the school. Mark received his assignment and was sent to meet his supervising teacher. Marilyn's supervising teacher, Ms Conroy, wasn't in the building yet.

Mr. Bibs said, "I'll take you to her room. Just give me a minute to make a call."

Feeling uncomfortable under the gaze of Mr. Bibs, Marilyn said, "Okay, I'll wait in the outer office to give you some privacy." As Marilyn was about to open the door, Mr. Bibs pressed against her while opening the door for her. He apologized for being so clumsy, but to Marilyn, it seemed like his intention was to get him a feel.

A.J.'s Pursuits

The outer office was a bee hive of activity. Marilyn and the three clerks introduced themselves; as the introductions were ending Ms Conroy entered the office.

One of the clerks said, "Kathy; I mean Ms Conroy, this is your new student teacher Ms Marilyn Spears."

"Good to meet you, Marilyn. Forgive me for rushing, but I need some coffee."

They still had twenty minutes before class. Ms Conroy stopped at her locker, and then they went for coffee.

When they got to the cafeteria, Ms Conroy saw Pauline sitting alone just staring out the window.

Ms Conroy said, "I want you to meet somebody," as she led Marilyn to the table where Pauline was sitting.

"Good morning, Pauline. How are you today?"

"I'm okay, Ms Conroy. How are you?"

"Pauline, I want you to meet Ms Spears. She's going to help me with the class. You two talk while I get my coffee. Do either of you want anything?"

They answered almost in unison, "No thanks."

Pauline asked, "Are you a teacher?"

"Not yet, I have this semester to complete."

Pauline said, "Can I ask how old you are? You look so young"

"I'm twenty-two, and I have a five year old son. Here's his picture."

"Oh he's beautiful. You had your baby when you were eighteen."

"Actually I was seventeen. My baby was a month old when I turned eighteen."

Pauline's eyes lit up; she felt that she could tell Marilyn her secret. She said, "I'm going to have a baby too." Before Marilyn could respond to Pauline's news, Ms Conroy returned with her coffee in hand.

Pauline said, "It's almost time for class, and I need to get a book out of my locker. I'll see you two up-stairs."

Ms. Conroy looked through her school mail and found a copy of Marilyn's schedule. She said, "You have third and fourth period classes with me and then you go back to the college for the rest of your school day. Those are my two best classes. You'll enjoy working with them." Looking at the big clock on the wall, Ms Conroy said, "We should go. My room is somewhat isolated at the other end of the building." Pausing for a moment she continued, "I like it that way. Some people at this school I don't want to see that often."

The third period class ended and the fourth period didn't meet on Mondays and Fridays. Pauline was Ms Conroy's helper on those days. Having business in the office Ms Conroy left Marilyn and Pauline to attend to some class work. The two ladies continued their talk from earlier.

"Does your husband like being a father?"

Marilyn answered, "A.J. likes being a father, but we are no longer married."

Pauline asked, "Does your son's father visit him often?"

"Not as much as he should; there was a time that he saw him more, but I think he has found a serious girlfriend recently, even though he still calls me for an occasional booty call."

Pauline was shocked, she said, "You give it up and know he has a girlfriend!"

A.J.'s Pursuits

Marilyn was shocked herself having revealed such a personal matter with a person she had just met, but she felt comfortable.

Marilyn said, "Yeah, I still love him. I think we would still be married if my parents hadn't had it annulled. They said that A.J. was a playboy and they were right about that. A.J. never stopped fooling around and after I had the baby, he would spend more nights away from home than at home. I was only seventeen at the time and couldn't do anything about the annulment. My parents even suggested that I use my original family name, so I became Ms Marilyn Spears again."

Once again, the ladies' conversation was interrupted; this time it was the bell ending the fourth period.

The next two weeks went well. Marilyn and Pauline's friendship blossomed. As they talked one day, Marilyn's cell phone interrupted them. After ending her call; Marilyn took a deep breath and glowed as if she couldn't wait to tell a best friend a secret.

She said, "I'm going to see him tonight." It had been more than two months this time since they had done it, so Marilyn was looking forward to this.

A.J. picked Marilyn up at eight, but she had been ready since seven. When they got to A.J.'s apartment Marilyn was expecting to be fondled and touched everywhere until she was hotter than a firecracker. That's not what happened though. Instead she was offered a drink, which she accepted. A.J. started by saying, "I will always support our son, no matter what."

At that point Marilyn knew that A.J. was about to end things between them, she said, "No, I don't want to hear anymore! I'm not listening to you A.J." Then from her sitting position on the sofa, she dropped to her knees and crawled towards him. She was sobbing. She begged him to keep her in his life.

A.J. tried to comfort her having never said the words that he planned to say. He was going to tell her that he was going to marry someone else. Marilyn knew what was coming; she knew that she was losing him forever.

Marilyn stopped crying and mustered the strength to let A.J. tell her that he was going for good. After receiving A.J.'s parting speech, Marilyn didn't say a word; she just raised her tight fitting dress. For a moment, A.J. wondered if she was going to make him have sex.

Marilyn removed her torn panty hose and threw them in his face, and then she said, "Take me home you son-of-a bitch."

Marilyn sat by her son's bed crying most of the night, but she went to school the next morning. She was early; Ms Conroy hadn't gotten there. Marilyn had a key to the room now, so she went in to wait for the class. The first student to arrive was Pauline. She could tell immediately that something was wrong with her friend.

"You've been crying. What's wrong?" Then she remembered that Marilyn had a date with her baby's daddy last night. "Did he do something to hurt you?"

Marilyn didn't answer, but she did respond by releasing a flood of tears. The two women hugged, and even though Pauline didn't know what was wrong she too cried. It was as if she wanted to take part of her friend's pain.

"He's going to marry someone else", Marilyn said sadly.

A.J.'s Pursuits

"Oh, baby I'm so sorry," and then with more energy, Pauline said, "But he doesn't deserve you anyway! He's a damn fool for not realizing what he had."

Then she said, like a real thug, "I know some people who will kick his ass if you want them to and we can find his whore and kick her ass ourselves."

Despite her aching heart, Marilyn had to laugh at her friend's exuberance on her behalf. She said, "We can't make him love me."

Pauline replied, "That's true, but we can make him respect you."

The two friends decided to ditch school that day. They drove all the way to Milwaukee and spent the whole day in one of the world's largest indoor water parks.

With help from Pauline, Marilyn made it to the end of the week. That Friday they sat eating lunch in their empty classroom. Pauline, while rubbing her stomach, which was beginning to announce that she was expecting, said, "I have a big secret to tell you. This baby's daddy is a teacher here at the school. He'd be in a lot of trouble if anybody found out that he is sleeping with a student."

Marilyn was instantly alarmed figuring that a teacher had taken advantage of her friend. Pauline, as if reading Marilyn's mind, said, "He didn't take advantage of me. He didn't even know that I was a student." Pauline told Marilyn what she used to do on weekends.

Showing concern, Marilyn asked, "What does this teacher intend to do about this?"

"He says he wants to marry me, but I think it's only because I'm pregnant."

Marilyn said, "Whatever; it's his baby, so he's supposed to marry you. Andrew married me when he got me pregnant." That was the first time Marilyn had used Andrew's real name.

"My baby's daddy is named Andrew too." And then Pauline asked, "What does your Andrew do?"

When Marilyn said, "He's a teacher too. He teaches at Chatham High."

Pauline almost passed out. Marilyn noticing her friend about to fall rushed to her side to give her support. "Sit down. You look like you've seen a ghost."

Pauline looking in Marilyn's eye's said, "This is Chatham High."

It took Marilyn a second to comprehend, but once she did both women looked as though they had seen a ghost. They sat holding hands now realizing how much they had in common. Suddenly, Pauline took Ms Conroy's keys off the desk and just walked out of the room.

Pauline ended up in the girl's training room which didn't get much use that time of day; she and A.J. had met there before, but this time she wanted to be alone. As she sat thinking, she closed her eyes and remembered how things started. A few seconds later she felt his hand on her shoulder and heard him say I've missed you, and then he put his hand between her thighs. She resisted him but he was too strong.

She said, "Don't do that," and then she screamed but nobody came to her rescue.

A.J.'s Pursuits

Now sitting astride her to hold her in the chair, he taped her hands behind her back, and then he stopped her talking by taping her mouth; there were lots of rolls of tape lying around.

"Didn't you know it couldn't end like this? You can't get away with this that easy; I can't let you go like this."

His face was so close to Pauline's that she couldn't move without them bumping heads, so she could only communicate by stomping her feet, and that was hard to do with him sitting on her legs.

"Am I heavy sitting on you like this? Stomp one for yes and two for no."

Pauline stomped one time.

"Oh I'm sorry. I'll get up, but let me ask you this first." Their faces were now touching. "Was I heavy that first time that we made love? You're a bad girl, Pauline. You didn't tell me that you intended for me to make you a baby."

Pauline didn't respond.

"I missed your answer." He repeated himself but this time with more force.

Pauline stomped two times hoping to appease him.

"Good", he said, "Now let me make you more comfortable."

When he bent over to lift Pauline from the chair, she started stomping and kicking as hard as she could and ended up sprawled on the floor. She didn't know what was about to happen, but she was trying to prevent it.

"Look at you kicking like that with a dress on. It's so unladylike. I can see your underwear." He stood there looking at Pauline as she lay on the floor exposed. After a few seconds of pleasure watching her try to cover herself, he picked her up and carried her to the massage table.

He tied her down and had his way with her. As he was finishing he asked, "How do you feel? Latex condoms aren't so bad are they? You wouldn't be pregnant if you had let me use a condom." He removed his condom and went to dispose of it in the toilet.

When he got back to Pauline, she looked as though she was asleep. He shook her but got no response. "Wake up baby."

Pauline didn't wake up. She was dead. After realizing that that he had strangled her, he wrapped her body in sheets to dispose of it at the end of the school day.

After Pauline was disposed of, A.J. persuaded Marilyn to give him another chance and they lived happily for ever after.

A.J., with Marilyn by his side, opened the door to the training room. He called out her name, "Pauline. Pauline, are you in here?"

He said to Marilyn, "She's not in here. Let's go."

Marilyn walked further into the room and saw Pauline lying on the massage table. She shouted, "Here she is!"

The sound of Marilyn's voice caused Pauline to awaken. She had been asleep and had dreamed of her death. Pauline now focused, recognized Marilyn, and then she started to cry.

Marilyn went to her; she put her arms around her and said, "Don't cry."

Pauline asked, "Don't you hate me for what I did?"

"No I don't hate you," said Marilyn.

"But I'm pregnant with Andrew's baby; your Andrew!"

A.J.'s Pursuits

While looking at Andrew, Marilyn said, "He's not my Andrew, and I'm sure you didn't know he was anybody's Andrew."

Pauline only now realized that Andrew was in the room, she asked, "How could you do this to her Andrew, or do you prefer that I call you A.J.?"

Andrew didn't answer; he just stood there with his head down. But the momentary silence was interrupted when students began banging on the door. They were arriving for their workouts.

As they left, Andrew locked the door after them. He couldn't allow the students into the training room without a teacher. The students gave him a collective "Boo" as he walked away.

Pauline said to Marilyn, "I'm glad you woke me; I was having a bad dream."

Marilyn had been worried when Pauline didn't come back before she was supposed to leave for the day, so she found A.J. and they went looking for Pauline. As it turns out A.J. knew where to look.

That June, Pauline graduated from high school and her baby was due in a month. She gave up her apartment and moved in with A.J. Pauline's mother moved to the South to live with her brother.

Marilyn also graduated that June, and was offered a job at Jesse Jackson Academy, which she accepted. She would begin working in September and would be earning a pay check for the first time in her life. This was cause for celebration, so Marilyn called Crystal, who was home for the summer. They went out that night. They had remained good friends even after Marilyn divorced Crystal's cheating brother, A.J. Christian tagged along with his sister and ex-sister-in-law. He liked Marilyn, but she wouldn't consider the brother of her ex-husband.

That night, the three of them met Tony. Tony was a pusher, and even though he wasn't able to make a sale to his new acquaintances that night, he figured they were good for future business.

Chapter Fifteen

Life Comes Full Circle

That summer, A.J. was teaching a class for seniors who needed to earn a half-credit to graduate. He had handled the inevitable teenage crushes so far, but he hadn't met Jasmine yet. She wasn't actually a teenager; she was twenty year old and had dropped out of school when she had a baby at fifteen. Her daughter was now in kindergarten so Jasmine was able to go to summer school to earn the half-credit she needed to get her diploma.

In A.J.'s class, Jasmine would sit up front and intentionally expose herself to him. A.J. had changed her seat a number of times but she complained that she couldn't see the board or couldn't hear him and would always end up at the front again.

One day, Jasmine wore a short skirt and no panties. It was obvious that she wanted A.J. to see her jewel. She opened and closed her legs so much that she created an air flow. A.J. was determined not to succumb to this temptress. He lived dangerous though; he did look at what she was showing.

A.J. made it to the end of the summer without falling victim to Jasmine. She graduated and was no longer a threat to his creed as a teacher or his loyalty to Pauline, who had given birth to a boy a month ago.

September came and A.J. was beginning his second full year as a teacher. It was also the beginning of Marilyn's teaching career.

One day after work, A.J. stopped at the club for a drink. While he was sitting at the bar, she tapped him on the shoulder.

When he turned and looked surprised, she asked, "Don't you recognize me or do I need to spread my legs for you?"

"Sure I recognize you, Ms Jasmine, and your spreading your legs here will get you lots of attention."

"Did I get your attention, when you were lecturing to your class during the summer?"

"No you didn't; students don't excite me that way."

"Then I must have imagined the bulge between your legs. You looked so uncomfortable wearing your suit coat to hide it on days that it was 90 degrees."

She then leaned close and whispered in his ear, "It's doing it again." She pointed to his manhood, which had stiffened just from their conversation and perhaps memories. Jasmine patted him on his thigh and said, "Buy me a drink."

When Jasmine took a seat on the stool next to him, her short dress rose well up her thighs and A.J. could see her panties. It was like the old days, except in the dim light, he couldn't tell their color of her panties. He imagined them to be red. That seemed to have been her favorite color when she would treat him to the view in the past.

Life Comes Full Circle

A.J. wasn't the only one Christening the new school year that night. Marilyn was at the club with Tony. The two couples introduced themselves, and then Tony and Marilyn went to an isolated part of the club where some of the patrons smoked their private blends.

A.J. and Jasmine had sex that night for the first time. Marilyn and Tony also had sex that night, but it wasn't their first time. They had become quite the couple. Tony had introduced Marilyn to drugs and now he was her supplier and her lover.

A.J. and Jasmine sexual escapades were joyous for the next two months, but that joy ended when Jasmine told A.J. that she was pregnant with his baby. A.J. was mad as hell. He said, "Women don't get pregnant today unless they want to! You said you were on the pill, so how could this happen?"

"I don't know, A.J. I just know I'm pregnant, and I haven't had sex with anybody but you for more than two months."

"Damn, I don't want another baby; the two I have takes all I have. You need to have an abortion."

"I'm not killing this baby, A.J. I don't care what you say."

Jasmine was true to her word; she had a baby girl that summer. She and A.J. never stopped having sex. After A.J. got over his initial anger, his love of Jasmine's jewel dictated his actions. A.J. was now supporting two households. He was usually at Pauline's through the week and with Jasmine on the weekend. Pauline complained about him being away so much but accepted it; that's just the way it was.

Marilyn's drug use had increased to the extent that she had missed work a lot during the school year, and now that she had moved out of her parents' house, her son sometimes suffered from neglect. It became necessary for A.J. to take a more active role in Marilyn's life and the life of their six-year-old son. A.J. was now balancing time between three women. It was good that he wasn't teaching that summer. A.J. wasn't having sex with Marilyn, but he could; she was still weak for him.

Things changed for A.J. when Jasmine's oldest daughter got sick. She was diagnosed with a rare disease that was curable by the infusion of blood. Usually only one of the parents is suitable for the procedure; it was one of the dictates of nature. During the development of the embryo, a particular protein from only one parent is accepted by the embryo. In this case, it was from the father. Jasmine had been tested and proved not to be suitable for the procedure.

It was Tuesday, and A.J. and Jasmine had sex; the next morning, Jasmine was found dead. Her nude body was discovered by her five-year-old daughter, who called 911. Her mother had taught her what to do in case of an emergency. Jasmine had suffocated. It looked as though she was having sex at the time. Detectives couldn't determine if it was accidental or intentional, but evidence at the scene led them to question A.J. that same day. A.J. admitted to having sex with the victim, but said that she was fine when he left her at seven that evening. The children were taken to Child Services until relatives could be located.

At the time that A.J. was questioned, Pauline was out shopping. She learned of Jasmine's death as she was passing through the electronics' department of the store. Tears streamed from her eyes. She knew Jasmine well. Pauline's thoughts carried her back in time, and she recalled when they first met. They were both freshmen in high school at the time.

Jasmine had recently had a baby and was particularly friendly to Pauline. Pauline figured it was because they both had failed their first year, due to excessive absences, and were now repeating ninth grade. They became friends in a short time.

One day Jasmine said, "I know how we can earn some money"; she knew that Pauline was in need.

That night, they ended up in a motel room. Jasmine already had the key to the room, so they didn't need to stop at the office. They watched television and munched on the snacks that were there. Pauline had already figured that sex was involved; she knew that Jasmine had a sugar daddy. Pauline was so in need of money that she was willing to give up her virginity and trust Jasmine not to put them in danger with some psycho.

They hadn't been at the motel fifteen minutes when there was a knock at the door. Jasmine asked, "Who is it?"

"It's me."

Jasmine recognized the voice but feeling playful asked, "How do I know it's you? Give me a password."

Jasmine's sugar daddy said, "Love time," then he used his key.

Jasmine said, "Password accepted," as she turned and walked from the door. Pauline was shocked when she saw Jasmine's sugar daddy.

He hung his overcoat on the hook, and then he kissed Jasmine while looking intently at Pauline. He asked, "How are you ladies doing?"

He didn't wait for their answers before continuing, "You two sure look good!" He then took a seat in the one big chair in the room and motioned to Jasmine to join him. He pointed to the right pocket of his sport jacket. Jasmine knew the drill; she moved to his right side and took an envelope from his pocket, and then she gave him a kiss. He then motioned to Pauline and pointed to his left pocket. She was a quick learner, she moved to his left side and took the envelope from that pocket, and then she gave him a kiss.

Sugar Daddy said, "Jasmine, undress Pauline."

Pauline was surprised by the order. She turned away from Jasmine refusing to let her carry out the order. She was expecting to be allowed to undress in private and slip under the covers. He would then come in and do his thing, and then it would be over. The furthest that Pauline had ever gone was to let a boy play with her jewel in the dark, now sugar daddy wanted to watch while her best friend, a girl, undressed her. Pauline questioned whether there was enough money for that.

Speaking of money, she didn't know what was in the envelope. She had it clutched to her chest. She took a quick look inside. The money was easy to count. There were four one hundred dollar bills.

Before she could catch herself, she said, "Damn!" Then in silence she thought, this could pay some rent and buy some food.

Pauline put the envelope in her coat pocket, and then she returned to face Jasmine. "Okay, I'm ready," she said.

Neither of them had done anything like this before, but how much experience did a woman need to undress another woman. Jasmine undid Pauline's top, which buttoned down the front.

Life Comes Full Circle

She was wearing a black bra. Jasmine then undid Pauline's skirt, which when unzipped fell to the floor. She was now sporting a black bra and a white half slip through which you could see her blue panties. She couldn't always afford to be coordinated in her underwear, since tops and bottoms didn't wear out at the same time. Pauline wasn't about to throw away a good pair blue panties because the matching blue bra was worn out. Jasmine raised the half slip so that Pauline had to raise her arms to allow it to clear her upper body. This made her feel vulnerable, since she was unable to guard her most private part. Once completely naked, she stood there uncomfortable.

Sugar Daddy said, "Relax, Pauline. It's your turn now. You undress Jasmine."

Pauline was fast; she completed her task quickly, so that she wasn't the only one on exhibition. Now, they both stood naked and uncomfortable and Sugar Daddy was enjoying it. He became the director that would guide two inexperienced girls to what he perceived as stardom. When the evening was over, Jasmine and Pauline were well on their way to becoming the stars that Sugar Daddy wanted.

Pauline's thoughts returned to the present when a salesperson asked if she needed help.

When Pauline got home, her son was awake and hungry. A.J. said, "You're just in time." Pauline started crying again about her friend. A.J. asked, "What's wrong? Why are you crying?" Pauline pointed to the television that was showing a picture of Jasmine as the reporter told of her death.

A.J. thought that Pauline had somehow found out about him and Jasmine. He said, "I can explain about that."

Before he could explain, Pauline cried out, "My friend is dead. She's gone, and her poor daughter doesn't have a mother anymore. The reporter said she had another baby too."

A.J. said, "I didn't know you knew her."

"Yes I knew her well."

For a moment, Pauline's thoughts took her back in time once again.

She, Jasmine, and Sugar Daddy continued as a threesome for two years after their first encounter, but the ladies cut sugar daddy loose after that. They were able to make money dancing. Jasmine continued to get money from Sugar Daddy, since he was the father of her baby.

Jasmine and Pauline remained lover until about a year ago; Pauline wanted something that Jasmine couldn't give her.

Pauline's thoughts returned to the present when A.J. said, "I'm sure the children's father is going to take care of them now that Jasmine is gone."

"I doubt that Jay's father will come forward for her, and I'm sure he's not the father of her other baby."

A.J. said, "So you know him too?"

Pauline didn't answer the question before her baby demanded more attention. As she nursed her son, her thoughts carried her back in time again; she recalled when she found out who A.J.'s other girlfriend was. It was by accident that she saw him shopping with a very pregnant Jasmine. A.J. shopped with her, when she was pregnant just a few months ago at the same store.

Life Comes Full Circle

It didn't take her long to figure things out. She remembered her last night with Jasmine.

That night, with total dedication, Jasmine made love to Pauline. She had her climbing the walls; she didn't want Pauline to leave her, but Pauline said she had to go. Jasmine would have done anything to make her stay, but the one thing that Pauline wanted most Jasmine couldn't give her. Pauline wanted a baby.

That night, Jasmine vowed to Pauline, "You might leave me, but you will never be rid of me."

Pauline's thoughts returned to the present as her son became restless having finished nursing. A.J. took his son from Pauline and lifted him high into the air causing the one year old to laugh uncontrollably. A.J. thought about last night and his daughter and realized that he had to tell Pauline the truth.

He said, "Pauline, I have to tell you something."

As A.J. paused in preparation of his confession, Pauline thought in silence, *please don't say you killed her.* The ring of the phone interrupted them. It was A.J.'s six-year-old son. His mother wasn't home and he was hungry. A.J. had to leave to see about him.

When A.J. got to the house, Andy was watching television. A.J. said, "Hey, buddy; what're you watching?"

"It's Sponge Bob, Dad."

A.J. gave his son a hug and proceeded to the kitchen. "I brought you something to eat." It was Andy's favorite, a hamburger, fries and a chocolate milkshake. After eating, they sat on the couch and talked, but it wasn't long before Andy fell asleep with head resting on A.J.'s arm. A.J. put his son to bed and returned to the couch to wait for Marilyn.

Luther C. Grayer

Marilyn got home two hours later, still high from her drug session. She was surprised when she saw A.J. "What're you doing here?" She asked.

"Where have you been, Marilyn? You have a son to look after."

"Where is Andy? He's okay, isn't he?"

"Yes he's okay, but he was hungry."

Marilyn made her way to the couch nearly falling in the process. "Time just got away. I won't let it happen again."

A.J. walked to the couch; he was angry. He used both hands to pull Marilyn by her arms to a standing position. "That's what you said the last time you did this crap! You have to stop this!"

The sound was enough to awaken Andy, who came to investigate.

When he saw A.J. holding his mother, he cried, "Don't hit her, Dad. Don't hurt Mom."

"Andy, I wouldn't hit your mother. I would never hurt her."

Marilyn mumbled as she slumped back onto the couch.

"You wouldn't hit me, but you hurt me a lot." She then fell asleep on the couch.

A.J. put Andy back to bed and covered Marilyn with a blanket. He then took a seat in what appeared to be the most comfortable chair in the room, since he would be there for the night. The next morning, he got Andy ready and watched from the window as he got into the car with Christian. Marilyn slept through the whole thing. It was almost ten before she awoke.

She could see A.J. standing at the window sipping coffee, and then she remembered last night. Suddenly she thought that she was late for work again, but then she remembered it was summer.

"Where's Andy?" She asked.

"He's with Christian. Why don't you take your shower, while I fix you some breakfast?"

Marilyn said, "Okay. That sounds good to me."

A.J. had searched the apartment and didn't find any drugs. After Marilyn had shower, she ate the breakfast that he had prepared. She was then ready for other things.

"I need to go out for a while."

Andrew asked, "Where're you going?"

"I just need to go. I'll be back before Andy gets home. What time will he be back anyway?"

"He'll be gone for a couple of days, and you're not leaving this house."

"What do you mean, A.J.? Are you holding me prisoner? Do you plan to stay here and guard me all day?"

"Yes; that's exactly what I intend to do."

"I am leaving this house, A.J., and you are not going to stop me."

"You're not even dressed yet," and then with feeling, he said, "I know it's hard but we must do this."

"What we? I'm the one that's hurting here. I need something, A.J. Please, baby, let me go."

A.J. said, "It will get better and I'm going to stay with you until it does. Now sit down and relax because I will tie you up and gag you if I need to."

A.J. had talked to Christian, who was home for the summer.

He agreed to help. When Christian came for his nephew, he had brought the things that A.J. asked for. A.J. knew that a person couldn't be forced to sign into a treatment facility, but maybe he could keep Marilyn away from drugs long enough for her to begin to think clearer about what needed to be done.

"Get dressed. We can play a game of spades."

"I don't want to play no games and I don't want to get dressed. In fact I don't want anything on at all." Marilyn took off her robe and stood naked in the middle of the room.

"How do I look, A.J.? You used to like the way I looked, but you like the way a lot of women look, don't you?"

A.J. refused to look at Marilyn, so she bolted for the door. He got to her before she got there. He was now holding a beautiful naked woman in his arms.

"It's not going to work, Marilyn."

Marilyn was pressing and grinding on him while nibbling at his ear, she asked, "What's not going to work, baby?"

A.J. picked her up and carried to the bedroom. He placed her on the bed and straddled her. She now lay calm. That's when A.J. put the handcuffs that were already attached to the headboard of the bed on her right wrist.

Marilyn remained calm thinking that this would be a new way of doing it, but when A.J. snapped the second set of handcuffs on her left wrist, she got the picture.

"Don't do this, A.J.! Don't tie me to this bed!"

"If you make me, I will tape your mouth too." A.J. then covered Marilyn with the sheet, which she promptly kicked off. He said, "We have to make this work and your enticing me is not going to make me quit. If our having sex would fix things, then I would fix them real good. I know it's hard, baby, but we're going to make it work. I am not going to quit until you're okay."

Marilyn cried and kicked for a few seconds.

Then she said, "Cover me." After covering her, A.J. sat on the side of the bed and talked until she fell asleep.

Marilyn awoke a couple of hours later. She was wet from perspiration but was shivering at the same time. A.J. got towels from the bathroom and dried Marilyn's body. He then undid her right arm so that he could pull her to the left side of the bed where it was dry. He wrapped her in a dry sheet and held her close as they sat on the side of the bed.

Marilyn stopped shivering but complained of pain all over her body. She begged, "I need something, A.J.; please, baby." A.J. continued to caress her while promising that things would get better. She fell asleep again, this time in A.J.'s arms. He laid her down and she slept for another two hours.

When Marilyn awoke this time, she said, "I've got to pee."

"Okay, I'll get the pot."

"What? I'm not peeing in any pot, A.J.! Let me go to the bathroom; I've got to do more than pee anyway."

"No, I can't un-cuff you completely." He undid one arm so that she could get to the pot. "Here is the pot and the paper; I'm going to leave for a few minutes to give you some privacy, so you should do what you need to do."

Marilyn continued her plea, but A.J. didn't relent, so she used the facilities that he had provided. When A.J. returned, Marilyn sobbed, "Why are you cleaning up my mess anyway?"

As A.J. was walking away with pot in hand, he said, "Because I care about you."

They got through that first day. Marilyn hadn't eaten anything but breakfast and had thrown up a lot during the day, so she was hungry when she awoke the next morning. A.J. fixed and served her breakfast in bed, and Marilyn fell asleep soon after that.

As A.J. sat in the living room enjoying the quiet while Marilyn managed to sleep, the doorbell rung; it was Tony. A.J. had been expecting him since he had disconnected the house phone and had turned off Marilyn's cell phone. The only way for Tony to find out what was happening was to visit.

Tony was surprised when A.J. opened the door. "A.J., good to see you again; I came to check on Marilyn. Is she home?"

"No, she's not here. She's going to be in a facility for a while, so she won't need what you're selling anymore."

"What do you mean? I need to hear that from her."

A.J. made sure Tony saw the gun that was tucked in his belt. "You stay away from her when she gets out, or I will personally pay a dozen policemen to stay on your ass twenty-four hours a day until they get something to put you away for. You won't be able to make a dime in this town."

Then with great resonance, A.J. said, "You don't want *The Luke Grant Empire* on your ass."

"I just came by to see how she was, man. She's nothing to me." Tony then turned and left.

Later that day, Pauline called A.J. on his cell phone. She told him that the police were looking for him concerning Jasmine's death. A.J. didn't want the police to find him at Marilyn's house;

he knew they would force him to set her free. A.J. called Christian to come stay with Marilyn until he could find out what the police wanted.

Marilyn, knowing that Christian liked her, used her charm on him. "Let me loose, baby. It'll be alright."

Christian said, "I can't do that."

Marilyn now exposing one leg nearly to her jewel said, "I can't be nice to you, if you don't free me"

"Don't do this, Marilyn."

"Don't do what? I'm hot." She had now uncovered her other leg which caused her jewel to be completely exposed. Christian turned and left the room.

A few minutes later in the saddest tone Marilyn cried out, these handcuffs hurt! Christian reentered the room; he covered Marilyn with the sheet and started to adjust the handcuffs. As he leaned over, Marilyn kissed him on the mouth.

In an angry tone Christian said, "Stop this, Marilyn, or I'll leave these cuffs tight."

Marilyn said, "Damn; I thought you liked me."

"I do like you. I like you too much to do this."

Marilyn said dejectedly, "None of the Grant men want me anymore."

Christian asked, "Does Andy count? He wants his mother back. We all want her back."

Marilyn had another rough night, but Christian helped her get through it.

When A.J. went to the police, they arrested him. He was charged him with Jasmine's death. The detectives working the case figured that sex got a little rough and that A.J. killed the victim when he placed a pillow over her face.

While A.J. sat in a cell waiting for his bond to be made, he recalled what Jasmine had said the last night that they were together.

"I talked to Jay's father and told him what had to be done to save our daughter's life." A.J. got the impression that the father wasn't happy about the situation but that Jasmine wasn't going to take no for an answer.

A.J.'s bond was set at $150,000, which was arranged by his father, Andrew. A.J. told Pauline that he had cheated on her, and that he was the father of Jasmine's baby. Pauline thought to herself, *Jasmine targeted you; the same as I did. You didn't have a chance.* Pauline remembered what Jasmine had said during their last night together, *you might leave me, but you will never be rid of me.*

When A.J. went to Child Services to see about his daughter, he was told that the father had taken both children. A.J. said, "The mother said that I was the baby's father."

The person in charge wouldn't divulge the father's name but said, "We verified that the man who took the children was their father. He was on Jay's birth certificate, and he was legally married to the deceased which made him the legal father of the baby, since there was no other name on the baby's birth certificate."

A.J. was surprised to learn that Jasmine was married and that his name wasn't on the birth certificate. Jasmine had told him that she had put his name on the certificate. A.J. now questioned himself, *was she having sex with both of us? If so, we really don't know who's the baby's father.*

Even though they wouldn't tell A.J. who the father was, they did let it slip that Jay was in the Hospital to get the transfusion that was needed to save her life. That gave A.J. some relief as he left Child Services. At least Jay's father was doing right by her. She was where she should be now that her mother was gone; she was with her father. At that moment, A.J. had a flash back of good thoughts of him and his father when he was growing up.

When A.J. got home, he told Pauline what had happened. She too was surprised to learn that Jasmine was married; she knew that sugar daddy would never marry her because of love; she also knew that Jasmine would never have another baby with him.

Pauline asked, "How did they determine who was the baby's father?"

"Just the fact that he was legally married to Jasmine and there was no other father's name on the birth certificate."

Jasmine said, "That's not Sugar Daddy's baby, and if he married Jasmine, it's because she made him do it. Sometimes she just had to show that she was in control."

"How could she make him marry her? Who is Sugar Daddy anyway?"

To answer your first question, "She was fifteen when she had his baby; he could go to jail for that," and to answer your second question, "You work for the man; Principal Warren Bibs is sugar daddy."

A.J. didn't ask anymore questions. He made a phone call instead; He called his grandfather, Luke.

After the call, Pauline having heard A.J. on the phone said, "You're one of those Grants!"

Jay's father, known as Sugar Daddy, also known as Principal Bibs, went through with the transfusion. He was home recuperating when A.J. paid him a visit. At first, Principal Bibs thought that Andrew was just a teacher paying the principal a sick call but that thought quickly changed.

A.J. said, "Grant is such a common name, so you don't really know who I am. I chose a career outside of my grandfather's empire because I wanted to contribute differently to the world, but I assure you that *The Luke Grant Empire* is at my disposal if my family is in danger. You have my daughter and I want her back."

This was the second time that A.J. had evoked the name of his grandfather to seal a deal. Bibs stood motionless looking at the floor thinking his secrets had been exposed.

He burst into tears and sobbed, "I didn't mean to do it. I didn't mean to kill her."

Bibs later confessed to the police that he had smothered Jasmine while raping her. He said, "The pillow was to stop her from screaming."

That wasn't Bibs' only secret. It was learned that he was a pedophile that had preyed on students since the beginning of his teaching career and now he was going to jail for it.

Jasmine's mother took her children, but when DNA test proved that A.J. was the baby's father, he was granted custody of his daughter.

Later that week, Marilyn signed herself into Haven House,

a treatment facility outside of Chicago, and at the end of the summer, she was released. Christian, A.J., and Pauline picked her up from the facility. They had been her support team since she signed herself in ten weeks ago.

Who knows what's going to happen among these four people in the future? I have my ideas, but to know for sure what happens, I'll just have to wait to see.

What I can report now is that there was a party that Fall to celebrate the birthday of the family patriarch. Luke Grant, Sr. was eighty-seven years old. He had out-lived the five women that bore him seven children. He had been involved with two of those women at the same time for quite a few years. Andrew's life mimicked the life of his father. He too had seven children by five different women, and like his father, he was involved with more than one of those women at the same time. Of Andrew's seven children, the one whose life most mimics his, so far, is Andrew Jr. (commonly known as A.J.). He only has four children by four women at this time, but he is only twenty-six years old.

Life continues and what happens in the future might be worth reporting, but that's all for this story.

THE END

Printed in the United States
151291LV00002B/6/P